GIRL
IN THE
ATTIC

Dan
Djurdjevic

Pikkeljig Press

First edition 2016

Pikkeljig Press
PO Box 388
Bayswater 6933 Australia

www.pikkeljig.com

Cover photograph by Karl-Heinz Spremberg
Back cover photograph of author by Peta Santoro

ISBN-13: 978-0987623393
ISBN-10: 0987623397

For Maya and Lara

Mine

It was late Friday. Valentino's Ristorante and Pizzeria had closed but Rose was still in the bathroom, trying to wash the smell of onion and garlic butter off her hands. Of course she couldn't. The smell lingered even though she'd scrubbed her fingers until they started bleeding (again). In the end Rose gave up and dried her hands, surveying the fresh cuts that had opened up on the edges of her fingernails: long thin slices that went deep into her pink flesh.

Finally, she looked up at her reflection. The bags under her eyes showed the world that she was tired: tired in that bone-deep way only those who work all night on their feet can understand. It was the type of tiredness you got from rushing from table to table, trying to please customers who were cranky after a week of work or uni or school or whatever. It was also the tiredness you felt when your boss never stopped glaring at you from under his dark, bushy eyebrows.

Here's the thing about her boss, Sam: he hated Rose. In his eyes, she couldn't do anything properly. The more Sam expected Rose to stuff up, the more she did exactly that. She would drop plates. She would mix up orders. She would forget what the specials were. All this because she knew Sam was watching her every move like a hawk – just waiting for a reason to fire her. That made Rose feel like she was doing exams each and every Friday. And if there was one thing Rose didn't handle very well, it was exams. Assignments, fine. Exams, not so much.

But hey, she wasn't doing this work for the love of it. She needed the money. Boy, did she need the money. She sure as hell wasn't getting any from her mother. Especially not now. Not when she was in such deep, deep trouble.

"Sam is looking for you," said Evan as Rose came out of the toilets. It looked like he had been waiting for her. Evan was a couple of years older – already in his first year at WAAPA where he was studying drama. He once invited Rose to watch him performing one of Shakespeare's plays. Of course she never went. She didn't have the money or the transport. Besides, she didn't understand Shakespeare. Who did?

Anyway, she didn't know what to make of Evan. He made her feel nervous.

Like now. He was leaning on the wall outside the toilets, wearing his usual expression – a faint smile (or was it a smirk?) hinted at the corners of his eyes but not his mouth. Was he laughing at her? For the umpteenth time, Rose wondered if Evan knew her secret: her dark, terrible shame. Evan's father was a judge after all – in the Children's Court, of all places. He would know about her for sure.

"Yeah? What does Sam want?" Rose asked. "I've got to get home. It's late and I've got to study tomorrow. I've got exams coming up."

"He probably wants to pay you."

She scoffed and said: "Yeah, right. That would be a first." Getting Sam to pay her wages was as hard as pulling teeth. Or something like that, Rose imagined – she had never had a tooth pulled out (at least, not an adult one).

"You know," said Evan, almost to himself, "I really think you should speak to Sam about the whole money thing. It's time you got a proper wage – one that's paid into your bank account, not given to you under the counter."

Rose didn't know how to reply, so she stood silently for a moment, leaning on one leg, her hands crossed tightly across her chest.

When she was first offered the job, Sam had insisted on paying Rose in cash. He said this was because he didn't want to pay tax, insurance, superannuation, blah, blah, blah… stuff she didn't really understand. The agreement was that she would be paid a little more in return. All of this was meant to be a secret. So how did

Evan know?

It occurred to Rose that if Evan knew about her 'financial arrangement' with Sam, he probably knew her other secret too. The big one. After all, he still lived at home – with his father, the Children's Court judge. Over dinner Evan might have casually mentioned a grade eleven school student named Rose Azzopardi who worked at the restaurant. Even though he wasn't supposed to, his dad might have filled in the rest of her story. Maybe by accident. Maybe on purpose.

Or maybe someone Evan knew at the shopping centre had seen the whole thing and told him about it. The restaurant was in the same complex, after all. He might have heard how the pharmacy staff had stopped and questioned Rose. How the police had been called. How she had been arrested for shoplifting. Again.

Maybe he'd come to snoop. Or gloat. Or both. Either way, it might explain Evan's 'secret' smile. It might even explain his sudden interest in her money situation.

Eventually Rose said: "What's it to you anyway?"

"I just don't think Sam's treating you fairly."

"And why would you care?" Rose noticed some spit flying out of her mouth as she said the last word and immediately felt her face starting to burn. She instinctively wiped at her mouth with her sleeve. The little bubble of spit was clearly visible on the ground between herself and Evan. He acted as if he hadn't noticed.

"Just trying to be your friend Rose," Evan said quietly.

"Yeah well, I've got enough friends, thank you very much. So mind your own business, okay?" With that she turned and stomped towards the back room where Sam usually sat doing accounts or whatever. She could hear that Evan hadn't moved and imagined his gaze, still boring into her back as she walked down the corridor.

The door was ajar when Rose came up to it. Through the gap she could see Sam sitting behind a monitor at his desk, papers everywhere, boxes of stuff piled up behind him. The room had that stale stink of skin, sweat and humming computers. Whatever happened, she knew she'd be washing her hands again as soon as she got home. She felt dirty just standing there in the stuffy air.

So she knocked – a quick little tap.

"Who is it?" Sam barked.

"You wanted to see me?" asked Rose, nudging the door open and peering around it.

Sam snorted – like a horse snorts. Rose could see the hairs of his bushy moustache move with the exhalation. Then he shook his head and waved her in. Rose felt her heart pounding. Was she being fired?

"Lucy can't make it on Wednesday in two weeks' time. The second of November. I need you to cover her shift."

"But that's a school night... I don't know if..."

"I'm not asking you because I want to. I'm asking you because I have no other choice. Everyone else has some lame excuse." Sam had put his elbows on the table and linked his fingers. He was staring at her through his bloodshot eyes. Rose couldn't stop staring at them – and his black stubble, his double chin and his curly mess of greasy hair. He looked disgusting – a bit like the Banksia Man from those kids' books her mother used to read to her (back in the good old days when her mother used to do stuff like that). Rose realised she must have been staring a bit too long when Sam abruptly slapped the desk, causing her to startle.

"So? What's it going to be? Are you also going to give me a lame excuse? Because if you are, I can tell you that this will be your last night here."

"I'll do the shift..." Rose spluttered.

"Good. You live to work another day. Now get out. I don't want to see your useless face until next week." Sam turned back to his screen.

"Um, Sam... I wanted to talk about the pay situation."

Rose's boss sighed, abruptly grabbed his cheeks with both hands and pulled them down, making his eyes look even more bloodshot than they were. At that moment, he looked like some kind of ghoulish Halloween mask.

"After all your stuff-ups tonight you want to talk money eh? What a nerve! Did I, or did I not, just tell you to get lost?" He pursed his lips, got up and pointed at the door with his stubby finger.

"But... I haven't been paid for the last two shifts..." protested Rose as she backed out.

Sam kept his finger pointed firmly and said, through gritted teeth: "You know the deal. See Sofia on Saturday morning and she'll pay you from the till. Now get out. GO!"

Rose hurried out into the corridor, dodged the stacked dining tables and pushed her way through the double doors into the fresh, cool night air. Only then did she allow herself to breathe.

Here was the problem: for the last few weeks Sofia, Sam's loud, fat, fake, wife, wasn't there on a Saturday morning. No one was. So it looked like Rose wasn't going be paid – again.

But none of this compared to the bigger problem of her court case for shoplifting. She'd already pleaded guilty. The sentencing was scheduled for Monday morning. This was her third offence and the lawyer – a grouch named Lane who worked with her mum – had been giving her the third degree. As if she wasn't getting enough hassle at home.

Which was where she was heading right now. What

was that old saying? From the frying pan into the fire? Rose took another deep breath of the fresh night air. It smelled like rain was coming. Good. At least it would be cooler. Anything to turn down the heat at home.

As she walked down the quiet, deeply shadowed streets of Mount Hawthorn, Rose tried in vain to see the time on her watch. Eventually she gave up and pulled out her phone. It was 11:55 p.m. Maybe her mother would be asleep, if not in her bed, then slumped in her chair in the lounge, an empty bottle of wine on the lampstand.

Rose already knew that you don't get what you want in life. But, as that old song went, she hoped she might at least get what she needed. Right now, she needed her mother to be passed out so she could sneak up to the attic and finally get some peace and quiet. Was that too much to expect?

Of course it was. Rose should have known it too.

As she turned the key to their front door she could see light from the lounge shining through the leadlight window. Then came a blur of movement in the hallway, distorted by the kaleidoscope glass. Her mother, Valerie, was still up. And that meant there was a very high chance they would get into an argument.

So Rose stood on the porch in the darkness, a mosquito buzzing near her ear, the key in the lock, wondering if she should go inside or wait a little longer.

Their home was one of those old 1930s cottages, built with a wide, sloping veranda and Gothic redbrick walls that were slowly crumbling to dust. Rose had always felt the house looked haunted, especially with its roof of mossy tiles and disfigured gargoyles – not to mention the tiny attic window which was framed in cracked, peeling wood. The spiked wrought-iron fencing, gnarled rose bushes and the dead jarrah tree in the front yard just added to the overall effect.

It had started looking even more haunted after her father, Tony, had left. That had been three years before. A lot can happen in three years, especially to an old house that is already falling apart.

Her father used to be quite handy. When they first moved in, he always seemed to be hammering, plastering or painting at the top of a ladder somewhere. Tony had even tried his hand at 'tuck-pointing', which apparently meant fixing up the mortar between the bricks and putting neat white stripes on it.

But, typically, her father could never finish anything. For example, he only did the tuck-pointing on one side of the house. And similarly, the attic was left in total disarray: a couple of the rotten floorboards were torn-up; a split bag of plaster was left sitting in a disintegrating wooden box somewhere in the middle of the room; and an ancient wardrobe and other odd bits of broken, dusty furniture were pushed into one corner.

The attic had apparently once served as an artist's loft. That's why it had a tap with an old enamel basin (still lined with smears of dirty paint) on one side of the window. Somewhat strangely, a toilet was positioned right next to it — as if this were a perfectly ordinary thing to have in an artist's studio. The far end of the loft was walled-off to hide a rusting evaporative air-conditioning unit that the previous owners had installed decades ago.

Tony had the idea of renovating the attic and making it his 'man cave'. He even wanted to keep the toilet exactly where it was. He said: "You girls can use the downstairs one — this will be mine." But aside from replacing the old air-conditioner with a new ducted system (Tony ran his own commercial air-conditioning business), he did little else to the space.

So basically that's why the attic was still full of dust and junk when Tony left.

And it would have stayed that way, except that early last year Valerie threw some sheets onto the single bed that Tony had put in there — and told Rose she would be sleeping in it until Valerie said otherwise.

That happened after Rose's first offence for shoplifting. She had walked out of the local BP service station with a can of Coke Zero and a Taylor Swift CD — without paying for either. Which was kind of weird because neither Rose nor Valerie owned a CD player. And Rose didn't even like fizzy drinks – or Taylor Swift.

The court had let her off with a warning, but her mother hadn't. Valerie told her she could choose either the attic or the street. Rose picked the attic.

She spent two nights up there. It was mid-winter at the time, and bitterly cold, with the cruel wind shrieking through the many hundreds of gaps between the tiles. On the third night, Valerie gave in and brought her daughter down. Rose remembered how they had both cried.

The second occasion had far more serious consequences – for Rose, Valerie and their relationship. It had happened eight months previously. Valerie made her spend two whole weeks in the attic: one day for every dollar value of the item she'd stolen (a cheap set of in-ear headphones from JB Hi-Fi). Again, the court let Rose off – but as you can see, her mother wasn't so forgiving.

When Rose was caught for her third offence, she didn't wait to be ordered up to the attic. Instead she just grabbed her journal, iPad and pyjamas and walked up the narrow flight of stairs to the trapdoor. She had been sleeping in the attic ever since.

That had been two months ago – Rose had spent most

of the winter up there. And it had been a particularly cold winter too. Yet still, there was no sign her mother was willing to let Rose go back to her bedroom downstairs. She didn't even dare ask.

Rose wondered if Valerie might let her come down after the court hearing on Monday. Part of her hoped so. Another part had stopped caring: in some ways Rose had gotten used to the attic. She had her own toilet and washbasin after all. And she had managed to dust all the surfaces (as best she could) and vacuum up most of the dirt. She had re-arranged the furniture and gradually taken out everything that was broken and rotten – filling the outside bin bit by bit until everything was gone.

Sure, the attic could be as cold as the walk-in freezer at Valentino's – or as hot as their garden shed in the midday sun (Tony's ducted air-conditioning only worked downstairs). And every night the wind still whistled between the tiles, just as every morning she was woken by the sharp rays that came through the very same cracks.

Also, the lack of a ceiling meant that she was constantly dusting and cleaning. And washing her hands…

But at least the attic had become her space – one she had created by herself.

Most importantly, it was a place where she could be alone. Her mother refused to go up there for some reason. This meant Rose didn't have to argue with Valerie quite so much. She certainly didn't have to watch her mother getting drunk every night. She could even close her eyes and try to forget the mess downstairs: the dirty floors, the piles and piles of unwashed clothing, the crumbs and dried spills on the kitchen benches and the permanent stack of dirty dishes in the sink.

In other words, as miserable as the attic was, it belonged to Rose: it was a place where she could draw and write in her journal, count her money, and imagine the day when she could move out of her mother's house.

Rose was thinking of all of this, still standing on the porch with her key in the lock, when the door was abruptly yanked open – hard enough that she almost fell forward into the corridor. Valerie was standing in front of her, a pale, scowling figure in the yellow porch light.

"What the hell were you doing? Planning on spending the night on the porch? I can arrange that, you know," she snapped.

The argument had begun.

Rose didn't bother to reply but instead tried to squeeze past her mother and hurry up the stairs to the attic.

"You are two weeks behind in your board. Almost three," said Valerie to her retreating back.

"Yeah well, I haven't been paid for the last few weeks,

have I?" Rose replied, turning halfway up the narrow staircase.

"Don't lie to me Rose."

"I'm not lying!" As she said this she threw her backpack down. It didn't fall down the stairs but something inside cracked. Rose hoped it wasn't her mobile phone.

Valerie sneered, crossed her arms and slumped against a wall. "You expect me to believe that?"

"Yes, I do actually. Sam keeps telling me to see his fat, lazy wife on Saturday. He says she'll pay me then. Of course she's never there."

"Hmph. When the hell are you going to tell him to stop playing games and pay you properly?"

"I tried to talk to him. Tonight. He basically just told me to get lost."

"Is that why you were late?"

Rose made an exaggerated 'sad' face. "Aww… was my mummy worried about me?"

"You're damn right I was," Valerie spat back, her voice slurring.

"Look who's lying now."

"Don't you dare try to lecture me Rose! Don't you dare!" Valerie had raised her voice so that it echoed down the hall and up the stairwell. "Not after everything you've done in the last year. Not when things have been so damn… hard!"

"Hard?" Rose took a step or two closer to her mother, her brow furrowed, eyes narrowed. "You think they've been hard? For who? You?"

Valerie seemed shocked by her daughter's advance and took an unsteady step backward. For a moment she didn't reply. Finally she said, in a quieter voice: "Look, I know you've been having a rough trot lately…"

"Rough trot? What are you talking about? Horse racing? Don't tell me you've started gambling – like Dad?"

"That's not what I mean and you know it."

Rose shook her head. "Oh I know lots of stuff. But you… You haven't got an effing clue. Have you?"

"Don't swear Rose," replied Valerie, pointing her finger.

"Well 'effing' isn't a swearword, is it Mum? It's what you say when you don't want to swear. Just like – oh, I don't know – the attic is the kind of 'home' you give someone when you don't want to give them a home."

"That's not true…"

"What's not true? That you just made me live up there – in that filthy, draughty little gap in your roof – through the whole effing winter?"

"Don't you try to paint me as the villain here! You're the one who's become a thief! You're the one who's brought shame on this house!" Valerie shouted back.

Rose walked up to her mother until they were

virtually nose-to-nose – till she could smell Valerie's stale red-wine breath. Her mother rocked back on her heels unsteadily. Rose tensed her top lip and hissed: "Fair enough. But I'm not the only who one should be ashamed. You tell me," she said, pointing up the staircase. "Who else would do something like this to their own daughter?" She paused for moment. When Valerie said nothing, Rose continued in a childish, sing-song voice: "Would you like to come up and see my room Mummy? I've made it nice and pretty. I've even drawn some pictures for you."

Abruptly Valerie stumbled, falling backwards and steadying herself against the door frame of the lounge entrance. She stuttered: "You – you – needed to be punished."

"But never loved?"

"I do love you Rose." Valerie's lower lip was quivering.

Rose scoffed. "Oh please! You have a funny way of showing it. Anyway, why won't you come up to the attic? I'll tell you. It's because you don't want to see how I live – how you've forced me to live. You're too ashamed. And you should be."

Valerie started to cry. "I had to do it," she said between sobs, wiping at her eyes. "It was for your own good…"

"How would you know what was good for me Mum?

You say things have been tough for you, but have you ever thought – even once – about how it's been for me since Dad left? Do you know anything about my life: what I've been through – what I'm going through right now?"

Valerie sniffed repeatedly and shook her head.

"I didn't think so." Rose climbed back up the staircase, picking up her backpack as she went. At the top she turned and added: "Don't worry, I'll pay you my board tomorrow – from my savings. And no matter what the court fines me on Monday, I'll pay that too. One way or another, I'm going to leave this place soon. When I do, I won't owe you a thing." And with that, she pressed the light switch on the wall, pushed up against the trapdoor and climbed into the attic.

Valerie called from below: "I don't know you anymore! You've changed – just like your father changed!"

"Have another drink Mum. That'll make everything better," Rose shouted back before letting the trapdoor slam shut.

The pang of regret was immediate – like a punch to gut. She didn't mean those last words. They had just flown out of her mouth. But there was no way of pulling them back in. Just as there was no way of undoing any of the other mistakes she'd made in the previous year.

Rose sat down on the edge of her bed and held her breath, listening to Valerie weeping softly at the foot of the stairwell. Eventually she heard her mother's unsteady feet shuffling down the corridor towards her bedroom. Only once she heard the sound of Valerie's door closing did Rose let herself exhale.

The first thing she decided to do was check what had broken in her bag. She unpacked it to find that her new drink bottle, bought out of her savings, had shattered on the inside. Why did they make the interior out of glass? It just didn't make sense: that was thirty dollars down the drain. Luckily her phone was okay.

She poured the remaining water into the basin and spent the next ten minutes emptying out the shards of glass onto a piece of paper. Even though she tried to be careful, she managed to get a piece caught in her thumb, causing a bubble of blood to pop up.

That meant she had to wash her hands immediately. And because Rose was Rose, she did it three times, drying her hands after each round.

After that, she pulled out the night's tip money. People didn't usually tip at Valentino's, but if they did, they were encouraged to put the money into a big jar at the front counter. That money would then be shared equally between the wait staff. Rose counted it: $12.15 – a good night as far as tips went, but peanuts next to the wage she had been missing.

She got down onto the crumbling floorboards and groped under her bed until she pulled out the small, lidded pot that she'd borrowed from the kitchen. This was where Rose kept her money. After adding the tips, Rose counted her savings. Three times. If she made an error, she had to start again. That was her 'rule': she had to get the same figure three times in a row or else... She didn't know. It was the same as her other compulsions. She didn't even want to think what might happen if she broke one of these 'rules'. Whatever it was, it was sure to be something horrible.

When she was finished, she started getting ready for bed. Normally she might sneak down for a shower once Valerie's sonorous snores could be heard vibrating through the ceiling. This usually meant her mother was in her deepest sleep and would be utterly immovable. But even though she could already hear the steady rasp of her mother's breathing, this wasn't a night where she was prepared to risk it. So instead Rose washed herself at the basin (just a hand wash – she'd wash her hair tomorrow when Valerie was out).

After brushing her teeth it was time for her 'nightly check': Rose would first go to the trapdoor to make sure the latch was fastened. She'd unfasten and refasten it three times. This would be followed by checks under the bed and in the old wardrobe – also three of them.

The last check was the one she dreaded the most: the

ventilation room where her father's air-conditioning unit sat.

When Valerie first made her daughter move into the attic the previous year, Rose didn't have to check the ventilation room – because at that time the wall separating it from the attic had been completely sealed. Oh, there used to be a door alright – but Tony had taken it out just before he left, replacing it with a smooth particle-board panel (which he then painted, along with the rest of the wall, in a ghastly shade of 'peach' from an old paint can the previous owners had left in the shed).

Why? Her father had said he was 'renovating his man cave' – which, on reflection, didn't make any sense at all. But neither Valerie nor Rose thought much about it at the time. They had bigger problems: Tony's gambling addiction was one; the fact that he soon left his wife and daughter was another. In fact he left them the day after he finished painting the newly-installed panel. Valerie now saw the whole thing as some sort of act of spiteful vandalism. Or madness. Or both.

Anyway, the sealed wall only became an issue when, on the most recent new year's day – one of the hottest days of summer – the air-conditioning broke down, and Valerie had to call repairers (at triple their usual rate). They had to cut a hole in the panel just to get to the unit. Valerie asked them to install a new door, which they did (at an inflated price).

That was how Rose came to have one extra place to check every night.

On this occasion (like all the others), she gingerly pulled the handle on the door and, with trembling hands, shone her torch beam around the tiny space from just outside the entrance (she never went in). Of course, nothing was in there other than the box-like air-conditioning unit and its large aluminium foil vent. She closed the door and repeated the check twice more.

Finally she had to wash her hands again. Only then was Rose Azzopardi ready for bed.

She owned her money. She owned the attic (for now). And she owned her compulsions – but they also owned her.

Sparks

The air in the corridor at the Children's Court had the same stuffy feel as Sam's office, and Rose could feel sweat trickling under each of her armpits. Her lawyer, Lane, had told her to 'dress up', so she'd put on her best long-sleeved blouse. But the airlessness – and her nerves – meant wet circles were now rapidly expanding under her arms: she would have to keep them plastered to her body to avoid anyone noticing. She wondered if she was starting to smell and tried to sniff herself unobtrusively; yes, she was – despite compulsive washing, a ton of deodorant and more than a dash of perfume. It must be the stress hormones, she thought.

Rose looked around the waiting area. On one side of the room she could see a couple of boys with plaited rat's tails who were swearing and jostling each other while their thin, leathery-skinned mother perched stiffly on the edge of her chair, staring straight ahead with her lips pursed.

Opposite them sat a boy of about her own age. He was frowning as he pored over something on his phone, a dark smear of unshaven fluff on his upper lip and a peaked cap pulled squarely down over his heavy brow.

On the other side of the room, an entire family seemed perfectly comfortable in the hard, narrow plastic chairs – the parents slouched nonchalantly, picking their noses and reading ancient Time and National Geographic magazines, while their eldest boy and girl (twins?) alternately pinched and punched each other. Their toddler (a girl with a long line of yellow-green snot hanging from one nostril) kept staring unblinkingly at Rose.

Where was Lane?

Rose and Valerie had managed to avoid each other for almost the entire weekend – not counting the odd, uncomfortable, encounter in the hallway.

On the last of these, on Sunday, her mother had spoken as Rose squeezed past her, saying:

"You all set for court tomorrow?"

"Uh-huh."

"How are you getting there – do you need a lift?"

"No, I'll be fine. I'm catching the bus and walking from the station."

"What did school say? Don't I need to write a note?"

"Mum I'm sixteen – they don't care about notes. I'll just turn up late and tell them I was feeling sick."

"Why don't you take the day off then?"

"What is this – twenty questions? I've got exams coming up – I can't afford to miss an entire day of school," Rose replied heading to the door.

"So where are you going now?" asked Valerie, but Rose just pulled her backpack over one shoulder and shut the door.

Rose had had some success with her pay at least. As expected, it didn't happen on Saturday but she finally caught up with Sofia on Sunday afternoon.

On both days, Rose had taken her human biology text down to shopping centre and sat in the shade on the edge of the rubber playground opposite the closed restaurant, trying to ignore the screaming of the hyped-up kids (and the tellings-off by the worn-out mums and dads) while she memorised the function of the human ear: tympanic membrane... malleus, incus, stapes... semicircular canals... cochlea and the cochlear nerves...

Finally at about 4:00 p.m. she looked up to see Sofia's bum wobbling as she struggled to unlock the front double doors. Rose closed her book and rushed up, narrowly dodging a hyperactive boy who had managed to run under her feet. She got to the door just before it swung shut.

"Rose..." said Sofia turning around in surprise.

"I've come to sort out my pay. For the last three shifts." The door jingled as it closed behind Rose. Sofia went behind the till and put her handbag down.

"Three shifts? I don't think that's right."

"Yes it is. The seventh, fourteenth and twenty-first of October. I worked all three nights. I haven't been paid for them."

Sofia chuckled. "Someone seems to have their knickers in a twist."

Rose didn't answer but crossed her arms, hugging her textbook to her chest.

Eventually Sofia sighed and pressed the button on the till. "Okay then. So that's $17.70 per hour, for six hours times three…"

"No – I get paid $19.00 per hour."

Sofia laughed. "Sweetie, you're on the minimum. And from what I hear, you're lucky you're even getting that."

Rose walked up to the counter and slammed her textbook down on it. Sofia jumped back in surprise. "Sam and I made a deal," Rose said. "I get paid $19.00 per hour."

"Now why would he make a deal like that?"

"You know why – because he didn't want to pay tax and all the other stuff." Rose, who was now leaning on the counter and staring at Sofia, continued: "It's funny how you always used to pay me without complaining – but now you're trying to get out of it."

Sofia raised her eyebrows and gingerly reached into the till, flicking through the notes. Rose knew the restaurant was failing. This was most probably because Sam kept cutting corners. On everything. A lot of the food was stale. Sometimes it was 'recycled' from the previous night. Some of it was plain rotten. Rose didn't dare go into the freezer any more: boxes had been knocked over and produce had spilled over onto the floor. People would step on it and still use it for cooking. Other stuff that should have been in the freezer was kept in Sam's office 'because the freezer was too full'.

Bookings were down and every night there seemed to be fewer and fewer people at the tables.

"I'll have to go to the petty cash tin. There's not enough in the till," said Sofia absently as she turned and waddled around the corner and off to the office. She no doubt assumed she was out of sight when she grabbed the tip jar (still full from lunch – the staff were probably told it would be divided up 'next time') but Rose saw everything reflected in the wide restaurant windows.

Sofia was gone for what seemed like an eternity. And when she came back, her face was red – with anger. She'd obviously been talking to Sam on the phone. She was carrying a wad of notes which she slapped down on the counter in front of Rose. "You realise," she said, "that this is hardly legal."

"Tell that to Sam. I just want to be paid like everyone else."

"Don't worry," she replied with a sneer, "I'm going to

arrange that on Monday. And by the way, you'll be on $17.70 per hour. If you don't like it, you can leave. Otherwise, I'll need your bank account details."

Rose reached into her backpack and pulled out a sealed envelope. "Organised," she said.

Sofia sniffed and snatched it out of her hands.

Rose was mid-way through her third count of the money when Sofia, who was leaning back and smirking, commented: "I don't know why we bother to keep you on. As far as I can see, you're useless. You can't even add up properly. How many times are you going to keep doing that?"

Rose stopped counting and rolled her eyes. She'd have to start the whole thing again. But she'd do it later – when she was alone. "I'm triple-checking because I don't trust you. Just like you don't trust me. That's a choice we both make, isn't it? We both see what we want to see."

"What the hell are you on about?" asked Sofia frowning.

"I see how mean you are to me. I see how you won't pay me what I'm owed. I see you stealing money from the tip jar – like you did just then when you thought I wasn't watching."

"That's..." started Sophia, but Rose talked over the top of her.

"Sure, there are probably some nice things about you

that I choose not to see – but hey, that's just the way it is."

"You have a nerve talking to me like that! How dare you be so rude?"

"Because you're no different – it's just that normally you get away with it and I'm not allowed to. Notice how you only ever see my mistakes – the ones I make when I'm nervous? You choose to see them. But you choose to ignore the fact that the customers actually like me – that the regulars always ask for me. I mean, that's how you run your whole business, isn't it? You choose to buy all your bread cheaply from the bakery at the end of the day when they are about to bin everything. You choose to ignore the use-by date on the frozen tartufo and tiramisu. And you pretend that the pre-made bolognaise sauce in the fridge is still fine to use even when it has something green growing on top."

"Those are all lies!"

"Are they? Then why are all your best wait staff walking out? Could it be because they know a sinking ship when they see one? Of course, I need the money, so I'm sticking around – for now. And it looks like you're sticking with me. Unless you have someone else with experience in Italian food who can fill in for me – and for Lucy in two weeks' time?" Rose waited a while as Sofia stared at her, open-mouthed, then finished with: "Okay then – I guess I'll see you next Friday. Thanks for the money." Rose shoved the notes into the front pocket of her bag, grabbed her textbook and pushed her way through the front door. She was headed to the centre's toilets where she could count her money in private. And wash her hands.

The reason both Sofia and Valerie were so surprised by Rose's outbursts is that they seemed totally out of character. Rose wasn't usually the type to talk back. She might run away. She might cry. She would always sulk. But she never fought back.

Yet here was a new Rose – one who had fought back twice in one weekend. Rose rather liked her new self. She wondered if her outbursts might be sparks lighting a new future. Or was she about to burn down the house? Everything depended on what happened next.

"Okay – finally got here," said a somewhat out-of-breath voice and Rose was startled out of her daydreaming to see Lane standing in front of her, his pale, plump cheeks flushed red, and heavy beads of sweat welling in between the occasional strands of hair on his mottled scalp. "Sorry I got held up with a client. Are you ready Rose?"

She nodded.

"I see you dressed up like I told you to. Good girl. Now remember: be polite. And for God's sake, at least try to pretend you're sorry."

"I am sorry Lane," Rose replied.

"Eh? Now that's something I didn't expect to hear. All I can say is, you'd better hope the judge believes you. Come along," said her lawyer turning to walk into the courtroom. Rose looked up and saw that the clock above the door read 10:01 a.m. She hoped her case would be first up so she could just get it over with – one way or the other.

"Your Honour, as you can see, my client entered an early plea of guilty."

"Yes, I do see that. I also see that your client has been before me twice already on similar charges." The judge peered over the top of her glasses at Rose. "And both times, she promised me that I would never see her again."

"Yes, you Honour…"

"It's a very troubling situation, is it not, Mr. Bruckner? Ms. Azzopardi seems to be caught in a pattern of behaviour. And nothing I say seems to be getting through."

"Yes, it is troubling," agreed Lane. "Which is why I thought I'd bring to your Honour's attention some of my client's background issues."

"I'm sure I've heard them all before, but do go on Counsel."

"Ms Azzopardi comes from a broken home – a rather

unfortunate situation."

"So do many people," said the judge, shuffling some papers, "however, they aren't all shoplifters – are they?" She lowered her glasses to look at Rose again.

"Yes, your Honour. That's true. Her father has a gambling addiction which has worsened in recent years. He has left the family."

"So I remember." The judge had gone back to shuffling papers.

"Her mother has been particularly affected by the breakup of her marriage and has developed a drinking problem. A rather serious one."

"I'm not sure why you're telling me this Mr. Bruckner. It's nothing new. And it doesn't excuse Ms. Azzopardi's offence. It doesn't even help me understand why she did it."

"Well, your Honour, I'm trying to explain that she is a troubled young woman who is going through a very difficult time in her life."

"And what are all the shopkeepers to do while she passes through this 'difficult time'? Accept that she is going to keep stealing from them? Remind me: what did she take on this most recent occasion?"

"It was a selection of clips and hair ties from a stand in her local pharmacy."

"Is your client so poor, and desperate for hair accessories, that she needed to steal them?"

"No your Honour. That's the point exactly. You see, it doesn't make any sense at all. Ms. Azzopardi has a part-time job at her local restaurant, Valentino's…"

"I know the place. If I were a food critic, I'd give it one star out of five, but I won't hold that against your client."

"I'm much obliged your Honour," said Lane.

"Anyway, she clearly has her own money," noted the judge.

"She does. By all accounts, she is very hard-working, is achieving well in school and has a good sense of where she wants to be in the future in terms of a career in graphic design."

"Her mother is a lawyer, isn't she?" asked the judge, peering down at Rose again over her glasses.

"Uh, yes, your Honour…"

"Tell me then: why is your client making such a mess of her life?"

"Well that's just it: she can't help herself. She's acting out of compulsion. It doesn't make any sense, any more than her father's gambling or her mother's drinking."

"I can hear the violins playing Counsel but I'm afraid they aren't moving me."

"I urge your Honour to give Ms. Azzopardi one last chance. Otherwise she will have a criminal conviction, one that could affect her entire future – her career, her relationships and her mental health."

"She's had three chances already Counsel. Normally it's three strikes and you're out. Isn't that so?"

Rose could see a trickle of sweat running down Lane's forehead to the end of his nose. He wiped it away with his hand.

"Well… my client is very sorry for what she's done. She knows she has a problem and wants to do something about it. She wants to make sure it never happens again. That's why she is going to get professional help. She has an appointment with a psychiatrist regarding her kleptomania. In fact, the appointment is for this Thursday."

That was the first Rose had heard about an appointment with a psychiatrist. And she had never discussed kleptomania with Lane. She knew what it was, of course. When you're like Rose and you can't help stealing things, you start Googling to find out why.

The judge took off her glasses, cleared her throat and stared at Rose. "Thank you Mr. Bruckner. I'd like to hear directly from the defendant now. Please stand Ms. Azzopardi."

Rose got up slowly, feeling her legs trembling beneath her.

"Before I sentence you, do you have anything you want to say?"

"Um… just that I'm really sorry. For everything. I don't want to do things like that. I don't know why I do them. I want to stop. I will stop. I've already started changing my life, trying harder... organising things properly... standing up for myself..." Rose's voice trailed off. She didn't know what else to say.

"Ms Azzopardi, here's the thing: in the law we have something we call 'deterrence'. It's when people get punished to make them realise that there are consequences for doing bad things. Now I hear what you're telling me. And I think you really mean it. But if you aren't punished now, what's going to stop you going out and doing it all again – if not tomorrow, then in a week or month from now?"

"I won't!" Rose realised too late that she'd raised her voice. The judge, in turn, raised her eyebrows. Lane was wincing and shaking his head slowly.

"Oh? Why won't you?" asked the judge.

"Because I've already been punished – by my mother!" There: Rose had said it. There was no going back now.

"How exactly has she punished you?" The judge was now leaning forward, frowning.

"Well..." Rose glanced at Lane again and saw that he was squinting in puzzlement, waiting for her to continue, "when I first took the CD and Coke from the station, Mum made me sleep in the attic. The second time – that was when I took the earphones – she made me live up there for two weeks."

"Has your mother punished you for your latest offence?" asked the judge.

Rose nodded.

"You'll have to speak up so that it can be recorded," said the judge.

"Yes. I've been up there again since I nicked the hair clips. It's been about three months now."

The judge cradled her chin in her palms. "Okay – what is so special about this room in which you're being 'grounded'? Because that is what she's doing, isn't it: grounding you?"

"It's not a room. It's more like a gap in the ceiling. There's some old junk that's been pushed in there. And Dad squeezed in a bed. But other than that, it's filthy. It's freezing in winter because the wind... it just blows right through. I got so cold I couldn't feel my toes for weeks. Of course, now it's starting to get warmer. Actually it's starting to get too hot: there was one night last week where I felt like I was in a sauna – I couldn't sleep at all."

"Has your mother made any effort to make this space liveable?"

"No... I cleaned it as best as I could. But you can't stop the dust coming down. Or the spiders making new webs. There are rats too. I see them all the time." Rose heard her voice wavering as tears welled in her eyes. "And I get quite scared at night..." Abruptly she started to cry. She stood there sobbing for a while, covering her eyes. Between her fingers, and through the hot film of tears, she could see the judge waving for her to sit, then felt the gentle hand of the usher guiding her down.

"Counsel will please rise," said the judge, and Lane stood up straightening his jacket.

"This is very disturbing. Were you aware of your client's living arrangements Mr. Bruckner?"

Lane cleared his throat and said: "No, your Honour, I was not."

"I see. Okay… you may sit." The judge put her glasses back on and thumbed through her pages, found the one she was looking for and started writing notes. This went on for some time.

Finally the judge finished, took off her glasses and looked up, saying: "Will the defendant please stand… Rose Azzopardi, I find you guilty of stealing. I accept that you are genuinely sorry for what you've done. And it seems you have already been punished – quite severely in fact – by your mother. In those circumstances I'm going to give you just one more chance. But I'm giving it to you on two very strict conditions. The first is that you must attend fortnightly sessions with your psychiatrist for at least two months from today. The second condition is that you will be grounded for two more months – which means no going out to parties or visiting friends. However, you will be grounded in your own bedroom – not in this 'attic' that you have told me about. Do you understand everything that I've just said?"

Rose nodded.

"And do you agree to those conditions?"

Rose nodded again.

"Let the record show that the defendant has indicated yes," said the judge. She turned to Lane. "Now – Mr. Bruckner…"

"Your Honour," he said, jumping to his feet.

"I am very disturbed by what we have heard this morning – and greatly concerned that you apparently knew nothing about any of it."

"I apologise, your Honour."

"I'm afraid that isn't good enough Counsel. You obviously didn't ask your client the most basic questions. I'm very tempted to report you to the Legal Practice Board. Luckily for you, I won't. Not this time. Just make sure it never happens again."

"Yes, your Honour," said Lane. He was sweating so much that his collar had gone dark from being soaked right through.

"And you can tell your client's mother to expect a call from the Department of Family and Children's Services." The judge straightened her papers and stood up. "This matter is adjourned."

"All rise!" called the usher.

Outside the court building, Lane rested in the shade with his eyes closed, breathing deeply and rhythmically. Rose was standing next to him clutching her bag, unsure of what to do.

Finally she asked: "Are you okay Lane?"

He opened his eyes and looked at her. "Why didn't you tell me what was going on at home?"

"I don't know. It didn't seem important."

"Are you kidding me? You saw what happened in there! I almost got disbarred!"

"Sorry."

"And your mother… Well, she'll find out soon enough." Lane took another deep breath. Abruptly he reached into his jacket pocket and pulled out a business card which he thrust at Rose.

It read: 'Patricia Clarke – Psychiatrist'. The address was in West Perth (not far from home – Rose could cycle there).

"I've already made an appointment for you," said Lane, motioning for her to turn the card around. On the flip side he'd written 'Thursday 28 October @ 5.00 p.m'. "You'll need a GP referral. Organise that as soon as possible – okay?"

"Sure. Um, thanks… for everything. I don't know what to say…"

"Just don't call me again. Tell your mother that she's used up all her favours." And with that he turned and walked away, the strands of his greying hair flying loosely in the breeze.

Rose felt like saying: "Tell her yourself – you work in the same firm," but she didn't.

Rose walked through the cast iron gate up the driveway to her 'haunted house'. She'd spent the day avoiding others at school but eventually her chemistry partner, Jen, (one of the popular girls) asked her why she had missed class. Rose had mumbled something about a dermatologist's appointment. Jen told her that, luckily, the teacher had decided to extend the deadline for their final assignment (which Rose and Jen were doing together). However, the class had gone through some important revision. Rose asked for Jen's notes so she could catch up and her classmate was only too happy to oblige.

Jen seemed to be such a nice person – so unlike the other girls in the 'cool' group who whispered and sniggered whenever Rose walked past. Rose often wished she and Jen could be friends. After all, they lived just around the corner from each other. But somehow that didn't seem likely.

Anyway, at that moment Rose had other things on her mind: she was hoping her mother wasn't home so she would be able to slip up to the attic quietly and start studying. It wasn't an unrealistic expectation after all –

her mother usually got home quite late from work.

Unfortunately she noticed that, even though it was only just after four in the afternoon, Valerie's car was already in the carport. Her heart sank.

Climbing the cracked concrete steps up to the porch, Rose could also tell it was going to be an awful night in the attic: the sun on her back was still baking the faded porch (and the tiny attic) like a blast furnace, while the air shimmered and hummed with the sights and sounds of approaching summer: blowflies, gnats and mosquitoes had created a cloud over the dead lawn, a dragonfly buzzed past (on its way to the Chiongs' pool, no doubt) and the cicadas were in full chorus somewhere deep in the overgrown lantana bushes.

Rose opened the front door to catch the sudden rush of cool air and the familiar scent of the house: dust, mould, ancient wallpaper and the faint, sickly-sweet memory of dead rats somewhere under the floorboards.

"Rose? Is that you?" Her mother's voice came from the lounge.

"Yes Mum," she answered, closing the door.

"We need to talk."

Rose sighed and pulled her school bag off her sore shoulders and sticky, wet back. An argument might be worth it if she could cool off for a while, she thought. Peering reluctantly around the door frame into the lounge, Rose saw her mother sitting on the old crimson velour recliner (Tony's favourite chair). Valerie's hair was dishevelled, her suit was crumpled and, of course, she had a glass of red wine in her hand – one quarter full and stained with lipstick on the rim. Behind her, the blinds and curtains had been drawn to block out the harsh afternoon sun. That was why the reading lamp had been turned on (although Rose knew there wouldn't be a book or newspaper in sight).

"How did your court case go?" asked Valerie.

"They let me off. And I'm not going to do it again, so it's all over. If you don't mind, I'm going upstairs to study now."

"Not so fast, young lady."

"Mum, please, just leave me alone!"

"Don't you want to know why I'm home early?"

Rose leaned on the door frame and crossed her arms, pretending not to care. But something inside told her this wasn't going to be good.

"I had a call today. From the Department of Family and Children's Services. You just missed them actually. They wanted to interview both of us." Rose said nothing, but suddenly felt a knot forming in her stomach and her heart starting to pound in her chest. Valerie drained her glass, took the bottle on the lampstand and, somewhat unsteadily, topped up her glass. As she did this she said: "You know what they said? They said that if you were any younger, they would have taken you away – but since you're already sixteen, it doesn't quite work that way." Rose felt her pulse quicken. Her mother continued: "All of which makes me wonder: what in the world did you tell the judge?"

Rose felt like she was in dream – one where she wanted to run but somehow couldn't move a muscle. "I... I'm sorry Mum," she said eventually. "In court... I started talking about the attic... It just came out."

Valerie shook her head, took a sip of the wine and said: "Can you imagine what it's like to have the government come around and tell you that you're an unfit mother?"

"The judge asked me some stuff... I had to tell the truth."

"Ah – the truth!" Valerie slurred these last words, some wine-tinged spittle flying towards the old floral carpet. "And so you told them I keep you locked up in a box – day and night?"

"I never said that!" Rose shouted back, hearing the tremor in her voice.

"Okay then – what did you say?"

"Just the truth!"

"Well, I showed them 'the truth'. I took them up to the attic. In fact, they insisted on it." Rose felt the pulse throbbing in her temples as her mother paused to take another sip.

"What did they say?"

"It wasn't quite as bad as they expected: at least it was clean and tidy. They still didn't like it though. It isn't 'fit for human habitation' – apparently."

Rose expected her mother to go on, but Valerie was now staring into middle distance, her wine glass dangling precariously from her hand at the side of her chair. Eventually Rose asked: "So what happened – in the end?"

Valerie drained her glass. "I got let off. Like you. It looks like we both had a narrow escape today." No sooner had Valerie finished her sentence than her eyes glazed over again. Rose waited for a minute then quietly turned, grabbed her backpack and was about to head upstairs when she heard her mother's voice calling after her:

"You should come down to your bedroom now."

Rose peered back in. "I know. I'll just grab my things."

"Do that. And you can help me make dinner afterwards."

"Okay Mum. I won't be long."

"Oh, and Rose…"

"Yes Mum?" she said, looking back in again.

Valerie paused for moment then said, as slowly and carefully as she could: "I didn't realise how much work you'd done up there. I think… you saved me today." Tears began to well in her eyes. "I… I'm sorry. And

I'm... proud of you."

Rose put her bag down, walked over to her mother, took the wine glass from her hand, and hugged her, smelling the acrid odour of alcohol mixed with Valerie's perfume. Her mother gripped her back tightly – so tightly Rose could feel bony fingers digging into her back and neck. When Rose finally pulled away, Valerie took her daughter's face in her hands and stared into her eyes. Rose could see the hot tears drawing trails through the make-up on Valerie's cheeks.

"We'll be okay Mum. From now on, we'll be okay. You'll see," said Rose quietly.

Valerie nodded. "Just promise me one thing."

"Sure Mum."

"When you come down, make sure that trapdoor is properly shut, will you please? I hate that place. And once you've cleared up, make it so we never go back up there again, eh?"

"I will. I promise."

Valerie stroked her daughter's cheeks with her thumbs and pulled her in for another hug.

As she climbed into the attic, Rose could feel the trapped, stifling heat and felt thankful that she would not have to endure it that night. A blowfly had somehow made its way in and was buzzing annoyingly around the room. That happened a lot.

Standing up, Rose had to shield her eyes from the blinding sunlight that cut straight into the room through the little window. She had to keep her hand up and squint as she made her way to the basin to grab her toothbrush and toiletries bag. After that she went to the old wardrobe and grabbed the clothes she had put in there. Rose kept most of her stuff in her bedroom, but her hands were still getting full: she'd have come back later for her pot of money and her journal.

She was about to head out, down the narrow stairs, when she decided to take a final look around the attic – the place that had been her 'prison' for so long. Rose vowed silently that she was turning her life around. And she'd help her mum do the same. Things were going to change – from now on.

It was then, standing in the alcove that shielded her from the sun's rays, that she saw the door to the ventilation room. The sharp sunlight meant she hadn't noticed before.

It was open.

Of course, it must have been the government people, having a look around, thought Rose. But why hadn't they shut it? They had probably just forgotten to.

With her heart pounding, Rose rushed forwards and slammed it shut. Then she hurried back to the trapdoor and climbed down as fast as she could.

She knew she was being silly, but still.

Conversations

"Tell me how things are going at home," asked Patricia. She insisted that Rose call her that (rather than 'Dr. Clarke'). She was leaning forward, resting her chin on one curled up fist. Rose could see the chipped polish on her fingernails and, somewhat strangely, dirt caught around the edges. Rose must have been staring because the doctor suddenly stretched her hands out, examined them and laughed – a gurgling, deep-throated guffaw – saying: "Gardening. I have Wednesdays off and I spent yesterday weeding and mulching." She clicked her tongue, still surveying her fingernails. "They're a mess, I know."

"I – I didn't mean to…"

"That's alright Rose," said Patricia leaning back. "So: how is it all going – really?"

"It's okay." Rose said, shrugging. She realised the doctor was watching her knee, which Rose was pumping up and down on the ball of her foot, so she stopped doing that. She'd been in with the psychiatrist for fifteen minutes already and they hadn't discussed the stealing at all. Patricia said she didn't want to get into that yet: this was just a 'get to know you' session.

"You don't talk much, do you?" observed the doctor.

Rose shrugged again.

"Any brothers or sisters?"

"No. Just me."

"And, I suppose, your mum and dad."

"No – Dad's gone."

"Oh… I'm sorry. Do you want to talk about it?"

"Not really," sighed Rose, looking out of the window. The sun had dropped below most of the buildings so the afternoon was looking grey and shadowy. It was even darker inside, but Patricia didn't seem to want to turn on the lights.

The doctor's office was actually a former bedroom in an old house that had been converted into medical consulting rooms. It was about the same age and style as her mum's place, except it was far better maintained: it had the same high ceilings, but here they were painted a clean, matte white, while the plaster cornices had been either repaired or replaced. And unlike the yellowed, wallpaper Valerie had on her walls, these were painted the colour of old bone-China, with framed Van Gogh prints (Rose loved Vincent's art) hanging from sculpted rails. Otherwise, the room was furnished with mirror-polished dark-wood cabinets, bookshelves that went to the ceiling and a neatly manicured fireplace in which a gas heater had been installed. Last of all, instead of the stink of rats and mould, this place smelled of books and freshly cut flowers.

"You know Rose, if I'm going to help you, you need to tell me a bit more about yourself."

"There's not much to say."

"Is your father still living?"

Rose scoffed. "Oh, he's alive alright. Somewhere. I think he's even still in Perth. Mum and I don't talk about him."

"He left you then?"

Rose nodded. "About three years ago. When I was in eighth grade."

"Did your parents argue?"

"Umm…" Rose thought about it for a while. "A bit. Not so much."

"So what do you think happened?"

"I don't know. Dad got fed up, I suppose."

"What did he get fed up with Rose?"

"Mum… Me." Rose suddenly felt tears welling in her eyes and she looked away to hide it – out the window to the golden light catching the tin roof of the building across the road. She only realised she was pumping her knee up and down again when she felt the doctor's hand gently squeezing it. When Rose looked back, Patricia was just a shadow, blanked out by the sudden difference in light. As her eyes adjusted, she could tell the doctor was both frowning and smiling at the same time.

"Parents argue all the time. And they split up. But I can tell you now: it's never the fault of their children. Ever. Do you hear me Rose? I want you to understand that."

"Yeah well," Rose said, wiping the tears from her cheeks, "it's not as if he ever wants to see me anyway. And I don't want to see him, so that's worked out well," she said, sniffing heavily. She was about to ask for a tissue when she noticed that the doctor was already holding a box out towards her, so she took one and blew her nose.

"I know you're hurt, and it doesn't make what your father did right," replied Patricia quietly, "but maybe he just has some problems he has to work through."

Rose laughed through her tears with a sudden cough and splutter. "Yeah. He's got problems alright: the main one is gambling. It wasn't so bad when I was little, but it started getting worse and worse just before he moved out. It was like he changed suddenly: he became more and more obsessed with horse racing. He started looking more and more tired – older, even: I swear his hair seemed to go grey overnight. And he stopped working. He used to do air-conditioning before that, you know? Ran his own business. He did well too. But he just let all that go: told clients to piss off, left jobs half-finished so a mate of his had to clean up after him. All Dad wanted to do was spend his days looking at the race guides on the net. Mum totally lost it. But stupid me: I was 'Daddy's girl'. I wanted to believe him. I actually sided with him for a while. He told me he knew what he was doing: that he had a 'cosmic formula' – that he was 'guaranteed to win'. And when he did win, it seemed to prove everything. But then he started losing. And he started losing more and more. Until one day I told him… some stuff. And he left."

"What did you tell him?"

Rose started crying quietly again, holding the tissue to her face and shaking her head.

"You can tell me sweetie. You need to."

It took a full minute for Rose to calm down. Finally she said: "I climbed up to the attic where he had his computer. He'd made this stupid wall a few weeks before: one that sealed off a door that used to lead to the air-conditioner he put up in the ceiling. The whole attic still smelled of the paint he'd used: it was so strong I could barely breathe. I found him at his computer staring at the screen, making notes in the book he used to carry around in his back pocket."

"You said something to him then?"

Rose nodded and smiled: it more of a grimace that lifted one end of her upper lip. "Actually I started yelling. I told him… I told him that he was throwing everything away: everything he'd worked for, everything Mum and I had worked for. I told him… that I was ashamed of him. That he was a loser."

"What did he do?"

"He just packed up his computer and walked out. Never said a word to me. Nothing. He walked past me as if I wasn't there. I stayed in the attic. I was too scared to come down. Then I heard him and Mum yelling at each other at the front door. Dad said he was moving out – that he'd take the van, but we could keep the house, Mum's car, whatever money was in the bank – everything. He said that he'd prove us wrong and that one day we'd want him back. But when that day came, he might not want us anymore."

The two sat in silence for a while, with Patricia nodding, making a few notes on a pad that she had cradled on her lap. She tapped her pen for a while before asking: "Is that the last time you saw your father?"

"Yes. Mum heard that he won a fortune on the horses just a few weeks later. Of course, he very quickly lost it all again, which was typical."

"Rose, you know that your dad has a kind of illness, don't you? It's not his fault and it's certainly not yours."

Rose looked down and nodded.

"What about your mum?" asked Patricia.

Rose breathed in jerkily, still wiping her eyes, before answering: "She drinks."

"Oh. When did that start – when your father left?"

"No – before. She's a lawyer. She said she needed it for her nerves after work. That was part of what Dad was yelling when he left. He didn't want to be married to a drunk any more. But her drinking has gotten a lot worse since then."

"I see… Is your Mum doing anything about it?"

Rose shook her head. "I'm going to help her though. I think she is just lonely, you know? And sad. She doesn't know what to do. And I haven't… I haven't exactly been helping."

"Your mum sounds depressed. That is a kind of illness too. People often drink or take pills to make themselves feel better. Other people… well, they have different ways of coping."

"Are you talking about me now?" asked Rose looking up at Patricia through bloodshot eyes. Her doctor had turned on a side lamp and was checking her watch. Outside the darkness was closing in.

"Yes honey. I'm talking about you."

"You think that's why I keep stealing things?"

Patricia nodded. "It's called kleptomania. It's a compulsion. You can't help it."

"How would you know?" Rose didn't mean it, but her words came out as if she were sneering.

The doctor didn't react to her tone. Instead, she said, quietly: "The same way I know that you wash your hands over and over again," and she pointed to Rose's red fingers and the deep, pink cuts near the beds of her nails. "And I bet you do lots of other things too. Habits you keep repeating. Little 'rituals' that you feel you have to go through…"

"I unlock and relock the doors three times…"

"Yes," Patricia said. "Things like that."

"You mean, lots other people do this stuff too?" asked Rose raising her eyebrows.

"Oh, you'd be surprised. Many, many people."

"So… what's the answer?"

"The answer is, we take it one step at a time. Understanding the problem is the first step to fixing it. And you want to fix things, don't you Rose?"

She nodded. Rose so desperately wanted to fix everything.

As if Patricia had read her mind, she reached over, squeezed her hand and said: "Don't worry – you will. You've already started. I promise."

Rose rode the back streets to avoid the peak-hour traffic, fighting the wind and the glare of the setting sun, as well as the steady climb uphill to Mount Hawthorn. She knew her mother would probably be home by the time she got back – but for the first time in ages she wasn't filled with a sense of dread at the thought of it. Sure, they weren't back to being 'close' – yet. However, at least they were no longer 'at war'. That was the main thing.

So instead of thinking about her mother, Rose let her mind drift back to the session with Patricia. Right at the end, the doctor had tried to lighten the mood – or so it seemed – by talking about hobbies.

"What do you like to do Rose – to relax?" she asked. "Personally, I like gardening," she smiled, raising her hands to show her fingers again.

"Um… I draw."

"Really? What kind of drawing?"

"It's nothing really. Scribbles."

"I'm sure they are more than scribbles. What medium do you use? Pencil? Charcoal?"

"No – ink pen usually. Just a biro. In my journal. I draw some pictures and write some stuff. I guess you could call it a kind of diary."

"I think that's wonderful. What do you draw?"

"Usually stuff from the day – or week: it depends on what's happened and how busy I am. It might be a design idea I've had – letters or a logo – or it might be a sketch of a place or person. Or it could be totally abstract – I don't know: it's whatever I feel like drawing at the time."

"Obviously you're reflecting how you feel at that exact moment. And that's really important – especially in the process we talked about – of 'fixing' things."

"Why is it important?" asked Rose.

"If understanding a problem is half-way to solving it, and the problem is the way you're feeling, then writing – or drawing – about those feelings can help you understand them. We call this 'cognitive behaviour therapy'. It's something you can do for yourself, by yourself. So you can see, keeping a journal is pretty much what I would have suggested for you anyway. Tell me – have you made any entries lately?"

Rose shook her head. "No. Not since before the court case."

"And why do you think that is?"

"I don't know. Oh wait…" Rose's eyes widened momentarily, then she winced.

"What is it Rose?"

"I left my journal in the attic, under my bed. Next to the pot of money I told you about."

"Why is that a problem?"

"It's just that… I hate going up there…"

"That's understandable. You associate the attic with a lot of unhappiness – feelings you want to leave behind."

"It's more than that…" Rose said, shaking her head. "I can't explain it. The place creeps me out. Especially lately. I feel like someone is up there – waiting in the cupboard or under the bed. Or in the ventilation room…"

"But how would they get there?"

"I know – it's silly."

"It's not silly," said Patricia. "It's called anxiety. And it's quite a natural reaction to what you've been through." Patricia paused and tucked her legs up on the chair (she had kicked off her shoes some time before). "Tell me more about your drawing," she said, changing the subject back. "You said you use a pen. What if you make a mistake? You can't rub it out then."

"That's probably why I do it."

"So that you can't go back?"

"I don't know – I hadn't thought about it really," said Rose tilting her head, trying to think of the words to explain herself. "I suppose I draw what I see. It's the moment that I try to capture. If I rubbed it out, I'd be rubbing out what I saw, and the picture would end up being something totally different – a different moment."

Patricia widened her eyes and laughed. "Wow. Then you must be good. Because I can't even draw a stick figure without wanting to rub it out and start again."

"Well… it's easy for me. I see a picture in my head and I just put it on the page. Then I write a bit about it – if I feel like it."

"Would you show me some of your pictures one day?"

"Maybe…"

"No pressure – only if you want to. And, by the way, it would be an honour if you would let me see them. In the meantime, I want you to continue your journal –

write and draw in it as often as you can. Do you think you can sneak up and grab it tonight?"

Rose nodded.

"Good girl," replied Patricia. "Now how about friends: do you have many at school?"

Rose shrugged. "A couple." She'd told Evan at the restaurant that she didn't need any more friends. The truth was, she pretty much had none. And it seemed from the sympathetic smile on Patricia's face that she had guessed as much.

"Okay, so what about pets – any dogs or cats?"

Rose shook her head. "No – we've never had either."

"Well then here's a suggestion: why don't you talk to your mother about adopting one from a shelter? Animals can provide a great source of comfort in times of sadness. For you and your mother. Worth a try?"

Rose nodded.

So there she was, standing up in the saddle as she climbed the last, steep hill to her house, her bike swaying from side to side, wondering what her mother would think about a pet. A dog maybe. Yes, a dog: a big one that could guard her as well as be her friend. She felt better just thinking about it.

Then she thought about the journal again – and the attic… Oh well – she'd have to dash in there and get it over and done with.

Rose could see the lights were on as she wheeled her bike up to the house. Valerie's car was in the driveway and she could hear bustling noises from inside the house. Normally their place would be in complete darkness except for a single, dull-yellow reading lamp in the lounge – and it would be depressingly silent – so Rose wondered if someone was visiting. But if so, who?

The warm smell of cooking (beef bourguignon?) enveloped her as she opened the front door. The noise was also suddenly amplified: she could hear dishes clinking, cupboards closing, the sound of her mother's footsteps walking from the kitchen into the dining room. There was even music playing on the lounge stereo: Leonard Cohen, her parents' favourite artist (the song was 'So long Marianne' – Rose must have heard it a thousand times in her childhood but this was the first time it had been played in their house for more than three years).

And everything smelled clean: an absence of dust, a hint of air-freshener, a trace of ammonia. Rose looked around and noticed the cobwebs were gone and the floors had been vacuumed – the hall runner had even been shampooed and was still slightly damp in patches.

Rose poked her head into the kitchen and saw that it too was spotless: the sink was empty, the surfaces had all been wiped clean, the dishes had been put away and the cast-iron pots and pans were hanging on their hooks. Through the oven window, Rose could see a casserole dish covered in an aluminium foil that vibrated slightly with the hum of the internal fan.

"Oh, hi darling – you're home," announced Valerie walking from the dining room. Rose could see the table had been set and caught the shadow of a flickering candle.

"Wow Mum. This is…"

"Something I should have done a long time ago. I know. Go and wash up because dinner is almost ready." Valerie walked up to her daughter and gave her a kiss on the cheek. Then she abruptly pulled her in for a hug. Valerie smelled of soap – not alcohol. Rose hesitated for a fraction of a second, then hugged her mother back, gradually increasing the tightness of grip. Was this the start of a 'new Valerie'? Probably not. But Rose was going to go with it anyway – for as long as it lasted. There had been too few moments like these, especially lately, and Rose was going to take them whenever and wherever she could.

"So I'm thinking of applying for jobs at other firms. I've got my CV ready," said Valerie as they were eating.

"Why Mum? Aren't you happy where you are?"

"Oh, it's alright I suppose… I just feel like a change. Maybe even a pay rise eh?" said Valerie winking.

"That guy Lane… he was pretty angry with me when we were outside the court. He made it sound like you two had barely talked about my case."

"Well we hadn't. I didn't want to be involved, so I left it to him. He owed me from when I handled his divorce. We lawyers do things like that for each other. I still think he got the easy part of the bargain. Family law is much more complicated and nasty than anything you saw in the Children's Court."

"Did you know Lane was going to book me in to see a psychiatrist?"

"Actually no. I can see now why he did it. I'm sure it helped get you off. But when you first told me about it I was furious. For the life of me, I couldn't understand why he'd organised for you to see a psychiatrist. It's not like you have a mental illness," replied Valerie. "You just needed somebody to talk to. You should have gone to a psychologist. Heaven knows, it would have been much cheaper: only one quarter of the cost." She picked up her glass of mineral water and took a sip. Rose noticed how badly her mother's hand was trembling.

"Have you spoken with Lane since?" Rose asked.

Valerie nodded. "Today. He said that this doctor you're seeing, this…"

"Patricia Clarke," said Rose.

"Yes, Dr. Clarke… Lane said she specialises in younger patients. And she doesn't just dish out drugs like most of the other psychiatrists. The bonus is, the judges at the Children's Court think she's the bee's knees. So I get why he organised for you to see her, I really do. It's just… she's so expensive. And with your father gambling away our savings… What I'm trying to say Rose is that… basically, I don't know if we can afford for you to keep seeing Dr. Clarke. I know it was one of the conditions set down by the judge but we just don't have the money."

"Is that why you're looking for a different job?"

"That's part of it," said Valerie, putting a shaking forkful of beef bourguignon into her mouth.

"Well don't worry about it Mum. I'll pay. Out of my own savings. I've got enough – for a while anyway."

Valerie smiled faintly. "Thanks dear. That will help. Just till I re-organise things."

Rose gripped both of her mother's hands across the table and stared into her eyes. "I'm proud of you Mum," she said. "You've done amazingly well today. I don't even know how you managed to fit it all in – especially with work. You should have left it to the weekend and we could have done it together."

Valerie smiled, released one of her hands and took another sip of the mineral water before replying: "No – I wanted to surprise you. I took the day off. I told them I had some things to organise."

"But you left early this morning…" said Rose.

Valerie was chewing again. She covered her mouth: "Yes – just a meeting that I couldn't postpone. But I came back mid-morning and I've been here since. I haven't stopped working until now."

"I can see that!"

"Enough about me," said Valerie patting her daughter's hand. Tell me how it went with your doctor. Was she okay?"

"Actually, she's really wonderful. I like her – a lot."

"I'm so glad. Do you think she'll be able to…"

"Get me to stop stealing?" Rose laughed. "She already has Mum." Then she got up, walked around the table, and gave her mother a hug around the neck.

Rose insisted that she clear away the dishes and wash them up, so Valerie retreated to the lounge. Except she reappeared at the doorway ten minutes later saying: "You know what honey? I'm so tired I think I'll go to bed."

Rose, who could see her mother's whole body shaking from alcohol withdrawal, just nodded and said: "Okay Mum. Sweet dreams." She knew Valerie had liquor in her bedroom. But this was her mother's battle to wage. Whichever way it went, she was proud of her: Valerie was trying. Whether she succeeded or failed in the longer term was a separate issue. The main thing was, Valerie wanted to change, just as Rose wanted to change.

And she loved Rose, just as Rose loved Valerie. They weren't exactly a picture-perfect family, but they had this at least.

Once she had finished up, Rose had a shower, taking ages under the hot jet of water. It was only then, while passing the staircase, towelling her hair, that she remembered her journal and pot of money waiting for her up in the attic…

The stairs were never designed to be kept permanently down. They actually folded away. Or at least, they used to – no one had tried to fold them up in years. Now they were so rusted-up that Rose thought they might break if anyone tried. And so they were just left there, blocking part of the hallway.

Rose had changed into her pyjamas and was cautiously looking up the staircase into the darkness. It was funny: she'd spent months going up to the attic every day and now, all of a sudden, the thought of climbing up the metal frame put butterflies in her stomach. How many nights had it been? Only three. And yet, the attic already felt like another world – a world that she didn't want to re-enter.

Downstairs Rose had a queen-sized bed – with an expensive, posture-supporting mattress. Upstairs she'd been sleeping on a tired piece of old foam – a single mattress her father had used before he even met her mother. Tony had constructed the frame out of recycled packing wood. It was meant to be a bed for 'occasional visitors'. But, in the last few months of their marriage, it had become Tony's bed again. Rose knew then that her parents' marriage was over. She remembered the day well: her parents had had a massive row: things were said: hurtful things that couldn't be unsaid, the staircase was pulled down and left that way. It was a reminder that their lives had changed forever.

When Rose first moved into the attic she could still smell her father – feel the dents in the foam left by his heavy frame. It had made her sad.

More recently she tried to smell the mattress but it just stank – a uniform smell of bacteria and fungi. Even the bumps had become formless: like a washing up sponge that had been used for far too long. Maybe Tony's 'spirit' had once filled the room but however Rose looked at it now, that spirit was long-gone. It had faded away – just like Rose's memories of her father were beginning to disappear. After all, Rose had tried to draw a picture of him a week or two before but found she could no longer remember his face – at least, not properly: not when they were happy and together. Since her mother had thrown out all the photo frames and deleted the pictures from the hard-drive, there wasn't even any way she could remind herself of how he – they – used to be.

Maybe, thought Rose, she was less afraid of what might be in the attic than what was missing from it. With that in mind, she began climbing the steps up to the top. Once there, she flicked the light switch on the wall, and pushed her way through the trapdoor.

As Rose stood up, she immediately noticed the draught. It felt as though the window had been left open – except that Tony had painted it shut (the wood had swollen too much for it to open anyway). The breeze was so strong that the single light globe hanging in the centre of the room was swaying.

Then Rose noticed the door to the ventilation room was open again, swinging gently on its hinges in time with the light globe.

Rose didn't wait: she dived down under the bed to get her pot and journal, only they were somehow just out of reach. She had managed to grip the journal by the tips of her fingers and pull it towards her when she heard the squeak of the door handle to the ventilation room. It was being pulled down. She froze. Then she heard the door click shut.

In a panic, Rose used her journal to rake the pot closer, grabbed both in her arms, and stumbled to the staircase without looking back. She pulled the trapdoor shut as she climbed through, slapped at the light switch on the wall and skidded down the steps, grazing her back and calves, and landing heavily on her bottom.

Back in her bed, Rose felt her heart still pounding, her bruises and grazes throbbing. She'd checked her room three times and yes, the lock on her door was fastened and no, there was no one under the bed or in her wardrobe. She was safe. So why did she still feel so afraid?

She finally settled her breathing and felt herself drifting off to sleep, focusing on her mother's steady, rasping snore through the walls. Somehow that comforted her.

Until she heard a cough – a girl's cough – coming from the attic.

Halloween

"We're Australians – we don't do Halloween. That's an American thing. I understand why the Chiong family do it: it's part of their culture – but it's not part of ours. You know how I feel about this Rose, God knows I must have told you a thousand times." Valerie slammed the fridge as she finished speaking. "Besides – tonight is a school night and you have exams coming up. There's no way that you can afford to be up late." It was Monday morning – October 31 – and Rose could tell by the bags under her mother's eyes, her acetone breath and the acidic smell oozing out of her pores, that she was hungover – as she had been every morning since their 'candlelit dinner'. It seemed the alcohol in her bedroom had provided too much temptation after all.

At least Rose hadn't seen her drinking as much lately. She hoped that this was because Valerie was cutting down – she was certainly a lot more irritable than usual and often very shaky. But maybe she was just holding out until she could get to her bedroom: Rose couldn't tell.

"I'd be back by half past nine Mum. And I'm up to date with all my studies. I really could do with the break." Rose was at the breakfast nook in the kitchen, eating Weetbix – with fresh milk for a change, not the usual long-life stuff. This was one of the many signs that her mother was making an effort: she had gone shopping. She had also done a few more loads of washing and another round of vacuuming. Rose had done her bit too, hanging the washing on the line, ironing and cooking dinner on Saturday night.

But her mother's drinking… that looked like it was going to take a bit longer to 'fix'. Rose wanted to suggest AA meetings or something, but she didn't know how to broach the subject.

"So where is it you want to go?" snapped Valerie.

"It's at WAAPA – in Mount Lawley."

"Rose, you're still in school. You've got no business going to a university function. Anyway, who is this guy who invited you?"

"Just Evan from work. I wouldn't be going with him, I'd be going with Lucy – Evan had two spare tickets and gave them to her." Of course Rose was lying here: Evan had given her a ticket on Friday night and said that he'd given one to Lucy the previous Wednesday – but there was no point in telling Valerie this because she'd throw a fit. So Rose continued: "Besides, it's not a 'function' – it's a theatrical performance. Evan's year is putting on a

Halloween special. We'd be in the audience watching. It's a family event Mum – not a party."

"Well I'm sorry – the answer is still no."

"Please Mum – I really want to go. It's not as if I have many friends. Lucy is really sweet – you'd like her."

"Lucy is also at uni. You should be making friends with kids your own age. Besides, I've made up my mind and that's that," Valerie said, the lines between her eyebrows deepening as she poured freshly boiled water into her cup of instant coffee. Rose saw the steam rising and curling in the morning light that scraped in through the window.

Rose shook her head. "You can be horrible – you know that?" she said, standing up and taking her bowl to the sink.

"I'm afraid that's part and parcel of being a mother," sighed Valerie. "Sometimes you have to be horrible in order to look after your child. Rose, you have exams coming up, it's a school night… I don't know why I'm having to repeat myself. Honestly, I'm sounding like a broken record."

Rose didn't reply but instead grabbed her school bag and stomped out of the room. On leaving the house, she slammed the front door so hard she worried for a moment that the lead light window might have cracked.

While walking from the bus stop to her school, Rose

kept going over the argument – and everything else that had happened in the previous few days. Thursday night had seemed so pivotal: she and Valerie had finally moved forward. But now it looked like they were taking steps backwards.

Then there was the stuff about the 'ghost'.

The morning after her experience in the attic, Rose had asked her mother whether she'd heard anything during the night. But, of course, Valerie had been hung-over and irritable: hardly in the mood to talk about her daughter's obsessions.

"No Rose. I didn't hear anyone coughing in the attic. What a stupid question."

"But I heard it Mum…"

"I suspect you dreamed it dear."

"I was wide awake! I had only just climbed into bed!"

"Well then it must have been the neighbours."

"No – it came from the attic. I could tell. The sound was directly above me."

"Rose, that's not possible and you know it. Let's stop this conversation. I've got a shocking headache," said Valerie, standing on her tip-toes to search for paracetamol in the cupboard.

"I know it sounds stupid – but I feel like someone is up there…" continued Rose.

Valerie found the box, fumbled it open and pushed out two capsules with shaking hands. "You used to make up dramas like this when you were in primary school but I thought you'd grown out of it," she said, pouring herself a glass of water from the sink. Then she threw the capsules into her mouth, took a large sip and swallowed, tilting her head back. "Come to think of it," she said, wiping her mouth with the back of her hand, "what exactly were you up to last night? You made such a tremendous noise you woke me up. It sounded like you'd tipped the piano over."

"That was me falling down the stairs."

"Eh?" Valerie screwed up her face in puzzlement. "Fell down the stairs? How..?"

"I went up there to get my journal and... some other things. I'd forgotten to get them before."

"Okay – so what happened then?"

"I was hurrying and missed a step... Then I slipped down."

"Did you hurt yourself?" Valerie was frowning and scanning her daughter from head to foot.

"I just scraped my back a bit. Bruised my bum. But I'm okay."

"Oh Rose! You can be so careless. It's because your head is always in the clouds."

"No Mum! Something scared me up there."

"Oh, here we go again..." Valerie rolled her heavy-lidded eyes.

"No really – the door to the ventilation room was

wide open. And then… it closed. Someone… someone pulled it shut…"

"Rose," said Valerie holding up her hand, "I've heard enough. You've always had a tendency to let your imagination run wild. You're… like your father in that way."

"Well who opened it then Mum? And who closed it?"

"It was just the wind dear. The sea breeze was strong that evening – don't you remember? It must have blown the door open, then slammed it shut again."

"But it was also open after the government people were here. There was no wind on that night…"

Her mother snorted but otherwise didn't reply.

"Did they take a look inside the ventilation room?" Rose asked.

"Who?"

"The government people Mum. Did they open it up?"

"Oh – I don't remember! Maybe. Probably. What does it matter? I had other things on my mind than worrying about 'ghosts in the attic'. I wasn't exactly paying attention to details like that. Honestly Rose: stop it. I've had enough." And with that, Valerie walked out of the room, heading to the laundry where she could be heard dragging clothes out of the laundry basket into the washing machine.

Rose wanted to point out that in all the months she'd been up in the attic, the wind had never once blown open the door to the ventilation room. And there was a good reason for that: it was fitted with a proper handle — a new one that had been installed at the start of the year. It needed to be pulled down in order to be opened. And Rose had slammed it shut when she was last in the attic. She remembered hearing the click. Or had she? If only she'd done it three times — then she'd know for sure.

"Hey Rose — hold up!"

The voice was Jon's. He had been talking with his twin sister Jen, and Rose had tried to sneak past both of them. She and Jen were writing their final chemistry assignment together and Rose was afraid Jen might ask how Rose's half of the paper was going (it wasn't — yet). Meanwhile Jon... well he never spoke to Rose at all, which was why she was fairly certain she had misheard him. Yet, when Rose turned around, there was Jonathan Chiong striding towards her, smiling broadly.

So Rose did the lamest thing she could have done: she pointed to herself while raising her eyebrows.

"Yes — you, silly! Who did you think I was talking to?" said Jon, laughing as he broke into a quick jog to catch up. Jen was suppressing her own smile as she followed.

"Um... Hi. What's up?" Rose asked, hearing the waver in her voice.

"Nothing. I just wanted to say thanks."

Rose frowned. "Thanks? For what?"

"For Saturday. My exhibition."

"Your exhibition?"

"Well, okay – it wasn't just mine, I know. Trust you to point that out," he said, laughing again. Jen giggled at her brother and made a gesture indicating that he just got burned.

"He's a bit full of himself, isn't he?" said Jen. Which was true. Both the Chiongs were popular, and they knew it – Jon more so than his sister. As far as Rose was aware, there wasn't a single girl in their year who didn't drool over him. Sadly, that included Rose.

"I didn't realise you were into art," said Jon. "I was quite surprised actually."

Rose wondered why that would be surprising. She also wondered what else she was supposed to say in this (very strange) encounter. It was as if the Chiong twins had mistaken her for someone else. Eventually she blurted out: "Yeah well… I sketch. I keep a journal…"

"Yes, you told us that on Saturday," interrupted Jon.

"We'd love to see it some time," added Jen. (Rose couldn't remember mentioning her journal to anyone other than her mother and Patricia – ever.) "And to think: all this time that you've been living around the corner from us, we never realised how passionate you were about art. Maybe it's because you've always been so quiet."

Or maybe you've never been interested in finding out

more about me, thought Rose.

But mainly, Rose thought about the oddness of the conversation. She had no idea what the Chiong twins were talking about. The best she could do was play along and see where it went.

Here was the strangest part: as far as Rose could recall, she had never once talked to Jon – other than to say "Hi" and smile weakly when he came to speak to his sister after chemistry (the twins took completely different subjects). Oh, and there was that time when Rose had run straight into him in one of the school's corridors. She remembered how she had fallen backwards, onto her bum, her books scattering everywhere, and how everyone had laughed, including Jon (although he had also helped her up and apologised, saying it had all been his fault).

"How did you find out about the exhibition?" Jen asked, her eyes widening. "You never did tell us."

Rose looked around for inspiration, wondering what to say. She couldn't very well tell them the truth: that she'd Googled Jon long enough to know that he was a finalist in the 2016 Emerging Artist Awards and that some of his work would be – had been – exhibited in the South Perth Community Hall. She'd even noted all the details in her journal (a good reason the Chiongs would never be seeing it).

Eventually Rose said: "Um… I follow the arts scene –

you know? I saw it was on, so I thought I'd... take a look..." Rose was flying by the seat of her pants, not wanting to sound ignorant.

"In that case, I'm pretty sure you're doing the wrong school subjects," said Jon. "All that boring science and maths... no creativity involved whatsoever!" He looked sideways at his sister with a smirk. She elbowed him in the ribs, with enough force to make him grunt.

"You just wait. One day soon I'll have a well-paid job while you'll still be working at the Dome Cafe," teased Jen.

Jon chuckled, rubbed his side, then turned to Rose more soberly. "I have to say – I didn't realise you dressed so differently after school." Out of her peripheral vision, Rose caught sight of Jen frowning at her brother and shaking her head slightly. Jon shrugged his shoulders as if to ask what he'd said that was so wrong.

"Don't worry about him Rose. He's a typical male," apologised Jen. "He doesn't know when to keep his trap shut. You'd think hanging around arty types would mean he would be used to people expressing themselves in whatever way they wanted." She was hugging a notepad to her chest. Rose had the same one, except hers was dog-eared while Jen's looked pristine.

"What... what was wrong with what I was wearing?" asked Rose.

"Nothing. Don't let him tease you," replied Jen. Then she turned to her brother and made a show of swatting him with her notepad. "See what you did? You're such a numbskull."

Jon dodged her swipes, grinning all the while.

The siren went.

"That's us. Better run," Jon said. He turned to his sister and said: "Remember we're going straight to Nainai's after school to help her with the food, so see you back here at 3:10 – okay?" She nodded. "Oh and Rose," he added, "don't forget about tonight's Halloween party. Our place. At seven. Be there!"

"I... I don't think my Mum will let me go."

"Are you kidding? Come on – you promised! And you can wear your 'after school clothes' – that way you won't even need a costume," he said walking backwards and bursting into laughter.

"Oh – go away you idiot!" shouted his sister. She quickly turned to Rose and said: "Don't worry about him. He's always teasing. He doesn't mean anything by it."

Rose puzzled over the conversation for the rest of the day. It made no sense at all. When had she supposedly gone to see Jon's exhibition? How would she have gotten there? The only way she could have done it was by bus. Rose could remember plotting the weekend bus route to the South Perth Community Hall – in fact, she remembered working it out in detail. But she also remembered deciding that there was no way she would be going to the exhibition. She wasn't about to embarrass herself by turning up to an event to which she hadn't been invited.

Yet the twins had made it sound like Rose had been there. And to make things more bizarre, she had apparently been wearing something outlandish as well. It just didn't make any sense. Was it all some sort of elaborate joke? No – Jen was a straight-shooter. And from what she knew of Jon, he was too. The Chiongs were so straight-laced it wasn't funny. For example, their annual Halloween party was always as clean as a whistle: no one drank or took drugs, no one smoked and everyone was out of the house by 9:30 p.m...

Okay – so Rose must have gone to the exhibition. She just couldn't remember any of it. But when had she gone? It must have been on the most recent Saturday – had it been the previous Saturday, Jen would have said something during chemistry class.

Rose remembered reading that the exhibition ended at around three in the afternoon. That meant she must have gone down either in the morning or in the early afternoon. Had she gone while her mother was out shopping? Okay, that was possible: there was a decent window of opportunity. But why couldn't Rose remember any of it – not a scrap? And what could she have worn to attract so much attention?

Finally, leaning against her locker at the end of the day, Rose felt a knot forming in her stomach and a cold sweat breaking out on her brow as she remembered her mother talking about Lane's involvement in her court case, saying:

'For the life of me, I couldn't understand why he'd organised for you to see a psychiatrist. It's not like you have a mental illness.'

Everything was starting to make some sort of sense. In fact, there was no other way it could make sense. It even explained why Rose felt like she needed to do things three times: deep down inside, she couldn't trust herself to remember what she'd done.

It was obvious now: Lane hadn't organised for her to see a psychiatrist because the judges thought Patricia was 'the bee's knees' – he'd organised the consult because he knew something was wrong, very wrong, with Rose.

She was at her locker, getting her bag, about to head home and the world started to spin around her. A salty taste came up in her mouth and her stomach started to heave violently. Rose dropped her bag and rushed to the toilets across the corridor, pushing through some girls from grade nine who swore at her. She skidded into the bathroom, scanned the cubicles, found one that was unoccupied and shoved her way in. She only just managed to reach the bowl as she vomited.

The world was still spinning as every successive lurch of her stomach lessened in intensity. She realised her nose had been running, creating a mucousy mess on her whole face, but decided to wait a while longer before wiping herself up.

So she knelt there, studying the pattern of the lumpy faecal matter stuck to the bowl just above her orange vomit, the hot, suffocating smell rising like acid steam in the tiny space.

"Rose — are you okay?" came a voice from behind her. It was Mrs. Mackenzie — her chemistry teacher.

She nodded and waved her hand behind her. But no — she was not okay.

The house was deserted and quiet when Rose got home: only the fridge could be heard buzzing in the background. Rose passed the stairs, paused to glance up to the attic and listen for sounds (there were none), went to her bedroom and closed the door.

She felt better: the bus ride home, together with the distraction of her phone and the internet, had put some time and distance between her and the shocking realisation she'd had at school.

Rose was even starting to put things in some sort of perspective. Okay, maybe she was sick — but so what?

People got sick all the time. Rose would just have to tell Patricia about it – she'd know how to fix everything: Rose trusted her.

Anyway, some people blanked memories out, didn't they? That's what seemed to happen in the movies. She must have embarrassed herself that Saturday afternoon – badly – and then pushed it out of her mind.

Sitting on the edge of her bed in the glare of the late sun, Rose decided that she needed to go to the Chiongs' party. She might get answers to some of her questions. The whole thing might even turn out to be a joke after all. She would have to sneak out when her mother went to bed.

One thing was for sure: she wasn't going to dress up. Yes, this was supposed to be a costume party but Rose didn't have anything that might pass as a Halloween outfit anyway.

Which made her wonder again: what in the world had she worn on Saturday? All black? She'd certainly done that before – black was meant to be 'slimming'. Yes, that must have been it. The rest had been teasing from Jon – surely?

So, Halloween or not, Rose Azzopardi was going to the Chiongs' party – in technicolor. She had her new jeans and the blouse she'd worn to court. Both were bright and, more importantly, both were conservative: even the twins' parents would approve.

The only problem was that when she opened up her cupboard, she couldn't find either of these items of clothing: she spent at least ten minutes rifling through the hangers but her jeans and blouse were nowhere to be found. And she knew she'd just washed both of them too. Maybe they were in the laundry basket? A brief search there also proved fruitless. Valerie would know where they were, decided Rose: she'd ask her mother when she got home.

But the rest of the afternoon passed without any sign of Valerie. Rose was just beginning to wonder if she should make something for dinner when a taxi finally pulled up in the driveway. Through her bedroom window Rose could see her mother paying the driver, opening the car door and, with some difficulty, pulling herself out. Then Valerie staggered along the path between the overgrown garden beds and climbed up the stairs to the porch, stumbling in her heels and fumbling with the keys. She'd obviously left her car at work because she'd been drinking.

"Rose?" called Valerie as the front door opened, her voice echoing in the hallway. The door slammed and Rose could hear the lead light rattle. One day it was going to break. "Rose – are you in?"

"I'm here Mum," she answered. She was lying on her bed with her books spread out – trying to complete her half of the assignment she was doing with Jen.

Her door opened a moment later and Valerie peered in. She was back to her dishevelled self: the bun in her hair had come apart and her jacket looked like it had been sitting too long on the back of a chair in some restaurant or bar. "You okay Pumpkin?" said her mother. She was in one of her 'happy drunk' moods (which were rare).

Rose nodded.

"What are you up to then – studying eh? Good girl," said Valerie, slurring her words. "I had a… work function. Halloween drinks," she said, waving her hand derisively, as if she'd been forced into it.

"I see you caught a taxi home."

"Mm-hm. Never… drink and drive. You know? Even if you feel like you can manage it, you just… don't have the… coordination. You know?"

Rose nodded.

"Well, sweetheart… your mother is going to have a little rest. Have you eaten anything?"

"No – did you want me to cook Mum?"

"Nah," said Valerie waving her hand and swaying slightly as she did so. "I ate all this stuff at the… place. You know? Finger food. I'm good. Did you want me… to make you something?" Valerie's eyes were drooping as she said this. It would have been funny if it wasn't her mother. Rose shook her head.

"No, I'll be fine Mum. I'm just going to eat some cereal in a while. I'll finish my assignment first."

"Of course. If you need me, I'll be in my bedroom – okay? Love you sweetheart," she said, blowing her daughter an alcohol-fuelled kiss. Rose smiled weakly in response and watched as her mother pulled the door shut, then heard her unsteady footsteps down the corridor. She was humming something.

At least she would be going to bed early. But just to be sure, Rose would wait until she heard her mother's snoring before slipping out.

Except the snores didn't come – not for a very long time anyway. This was because her mother mysteriously decided to try to sober up a bit. After only half an hour, Rose heard Valerie stagger out of her bedroom and go into the lounge. Then the television came on: the ABC news theme could be heard faintly through the wall followed by the newsreader's muffled monotone voice.

Rose tried to concentrate on her work, but it was almost impossible – she kept glancing at her watch, wondering when her mother would be going to bed.

And she'd given up on the idea of asking her mum about the clothes – Valerie wasn't in a state to remember anything. So instead, Rose had picked out her other jeans and a different top. They would do. Then she waited – flicking through her phone, watching random YouTube videos made by people whose lives were normal: funny and happy people. After that she browsed photos on Instagram of glamorous celebrities, cute pets (which reminded Rose to find some time to talk to Valerie about Patricia's idea – tonight wouldn't be a good night for that) and plates of gourmet food (which reminded Rose that she was hungry).

Eventually, at about half past eight, Rose stepped out into the kitchen where she poured herself some muesli. She ate this at the breakfast nook, leaning back occasionally to peer into the lounge where she caught the occasional glimpse of the television reflected in the hallway mirror. Four Corners was on. Rose could just make out the back of her mother's head.

She was considering going into the lounge to see if her mother had passed out when Valerie walked, somewhat unsteadily, into the kitchen. She had her eyes half-closed and was rubbing her temple on one side.

"I see you got yourself something to eat," noted Valerie.

Rose, who was washing her hands for the third time, nodded.

"I'm off to bed honey. I've got such a headache. I shouldn't drink at these work functions. They always ply me with too much."

"Should I get you some paracetamol Mum?" asked Rose, drying her hands on a paper towel – there was no point using the dishcloth because she would just have to wash her hands again after touching it.

Valerie shook her head. "No dear. I had some in my handbag and I took those. I just need to lie down now. How's your schoolwork going?"

"All done," lied Rose. "I might turn in early as well."

"Sounds like a plan. Goodnight sweetie," said her mother, swaying into the corridor, her white knuckles releasing their grip on the kitchen door frame a moment later.

Rose glanced up at the clock: it was 8:40 p.m. The party would be almost over. But the Chiong residence was just around the corner. Maybe she could still pop in once her mother was fast asleep.

However, it was already 9:10 p.m. when Rose, who had been pacing in the kitchen, finally heard the rasping sound of her mother's snores. She tip-toed to the front door, picked up her keys and gently unlocked it, then stepped out into the yellow light of the porch where she savoured the fresh breeze that was coming in off the ocean. Sounds of music and laughter were still coming from the party so Rose hurried off into the dark, moonless night.

She knew something was wrong very soon after she knocked on the twins' front door. It was opened by Mr. Chiong. He had been talking to someone inside, smiling broadly as he did so. But the smile faded into a frown as soon as he recognised Rose.

"Oh… Can I help you?" he asked. She tried to make out the tone: it seemed polite, but at the same time it was firm – terse, even. Over his shoulder, among the black and yellow ghoulish balloons and streamers, it was clear that people were already packing up and saying their goodbyes. In fact, most of the guests seemed to have left – these were just the stragglers. As if on cue, the music abruptly turned off. Mrs. Chiong suddenly appeared next to her husband.

"Rose?" she said.

"Um… Hi. I just wondered if Jen or Jon were around…"

"Well… Jen's helping her Nainai clear up at the back and… Jon's just gone into the shower. He's got an early start tomorrow."

Rose suddenly remembered: Jon was on the rowing team and had dawn training sessions a couple of times a week.

"Was there something you'd forgotten?" asked Mrs. Chiong, trying her best to smile.

Forgotten? Rose frowned. When she failed to answer straight away, Mr. Chiong sighed and walked away. Obviously he was going to leave this one to his wife. "No… It's alright, I'll see them at school tomorrow," Rose answered, backing away.

"Okay then. Be safe," said Mrs. Chiong, shutting the door.

And just like that, Rose was left alone on the porch, staring at a glossy poster of a carved pumpkin that had been taped over the Chiongs' lead light window. One of the cars on the road beeped as it drove away. Rose heard more people approaching from inside – happy voices growing louder in the hallway – so she slipped into the shadows and ran home as fast as she could.

Valerie's rasping snores could be heard from the driveway, but Rose was still careful to open and close the front door as quietly as she could, then tiptoe to her bedroom.

Once she was safely inside, she sat on the corner of her bed and pondered what had just happened. Mr. and Mrs. Chiong knew her well enough. They had always been polite, if not friendly. Yet tonight they seemed unhappy to see her – hostile even. And what did Mrs. Chiong mean by asking Rose whether she had 'forgotten' something?

Rose had a feeling she'd done it again. Maybe she'd said something rude or impolite to Mr. and Mrs. Chiong and then pushed it out of her mind. That must have been why they were upset with her. But when had it all happened? On Saturday?

Rose decided to have a shower and go to bed. There

was nothing else to do at this point. So she took off her top and jeans and opened her wardrobe to put them on hangers.

It was then that she saw her jeans – the new pair. And next to them was her blouse – the one she'd worn to court. Both were hanging in plain view.

Rose slammed the wardrobe shut and fell back on her bed, her heart pounding in her chest. After a moment she realised she was sitting on something – something hard and square. A school book? Probably. But why was it was it under her covers? She peeled back the duvet.

And saw her journal.

She hadn't touched it since she'd brought it down from the attic. Even then, all she had done was put it under her bed.

With trembling hands Rose opened up the pages, leafing clumsily through to the last entry.

Then, with a knot forming in her stomach, she turned over the page to see a new sketch – one that was clearly hers: she recognised her scratchy blue-pen style. It was a picture of Jon wearing a Dracula costume. It was dated 31 October 2016 – that very night – and was followed by a single word (in Rose's own handwriting):

'Halloween'.

Madness

Rose walked along the corridor to her chemistry class with her head down. Normally she felt invisible at the school, but today a murmur of whispers and laughter had followed in her wake wherever she went. In fact, it was happening to her right now.

"Oi Rose," called out Nathan, a boy from her class. She ignored him and kept walking. Nathan's group of friends sniggered. "Hey! I was talking to you!" he called after her. More laughter followed and someone said: "Freak."

Even people who were normally friendly to Rose looked at her quizzically – as if they wanted to ask something but didn't know how to bring it up. Of course, Rose had no idea what it was they wanted to say.

As she entered Mrs. Mackenzie's classroom she almost bumped into Jon again, except this time he jumped back nervously and eased his way around, making sure not to touch her. Now it was Rose's turn to call after someone: "Um... Jon..."

Jon however kept his head turned away, held his hand

up briefly to show that he didn't want to talk, then disappeared into the crowd of oblivious grade eight students who were streaming down the corridor, talking, laughing and jostling.

Obviously he'd just been in to see his sister, Jen. As Rose walked into the classroom she saw her trying to look busy, pretending she hadn't heard or seen what had happened.

"Jen," said Rose walking up to her. "Can we talk?"

"I don't think I want to," Jen said thumbing through her notepad.

"Listen, I… I think I did some things yesterday – at your party. But I don't know what they were. I want you to believe me…"

Jen stopped flicking through her pad and finally looked up, frowning, her lips pursed, saying nothing.

"Will you please tell me what's going on? I honestly can't remember what happened," pleaded Rose. "Whatever it was, I'm sorry. I'm really sorry."

"What are you saying? Do you have, like, amnesia or something? You know that doesn't happen in real life – it only happens in the movies."

Rose was aware of the others in the class whispering behind her, but she slid into the seat next to Jen anyway. "Honestly, I don't remember what I did. Okay, I know it was something bad – I just don't know what it was. All I remember is that my mum wouldn't let me go to your party. I finally sneaked out sometime after nine o'clock when she'd gone to bed. I walked around to your house and your parents opened the door. But it looked… like I'd already been there. I know, I know, it sounds crazy – but it's true," said Rose. "You have to believe me."

Jen shook her head. "That's the lamest story I've ever heard. I thought you were better than that. I thought you were a nicer person. And a smarter one."

"I'm not making it up Jen… really."

"You know how strict our parents are. But you turned up acting… like you did anyway."

"How did I act? Please, tell me," asked Rose, not sure she really wanted to hear the answer.

Jen rolled her eyes. "I could tell you'd been drinking. Everyone could."

"I don't drink!"

"Stop lying – it's embarrassing. And you know my parents don't allow smoking."

"I've never smoked in my life!"

"Oh please – I saw you!" Jen picked up her books and stood up.

"Where are you going?"

"To organise another partner for the assignment."

"But we're almost finished…" pleaded Rose.

Jen clutched her books tightly to her chest and stared at Rose. "I finished my half three days ago. Have you finished yours?" When Rose didn't respond Jen continued: "Exactly what I thought. I bet you've barely started." Jen turned to walk away. Then she abruptly leaned back towards Rose: "I knew you liked my brother. And the funny part is, I think he sort of liked you – especially after last Saturday. He thought you were interesting – different. So I don't know what got into you to come to our house like… like that. I especially don't know what you were thinking when you started… kissing him… You were all over him – in front of everyone. Is that what happens to you when you drink? I thought we were friends, but I realise I don't know you – at all. And I don't think I want to know you – especially after the other stuff I've heard today."

"Other stuff…?" asked Rose, feeling the world starting to spin around her again.

"Nathan's older sister works at the check-out in Coles. When Nathan got home from the party, he and his sister got to talking about you. She asked to see a picture, so he showed her last year's class photo. She said she recognised you – that you work at a restaurant in the same shopping centre. She also said she saw you getting arrested – for shoplifting."

Rose opened her mouth but no sound came out. The salty taste was coming up again.

"Tell me the truth: was that you?"

Rose nodded, feeling sweat beading on her brow, a thumping in her chest and her stomach started to heave.

"Well – from now on, I want you to stay away from me," said Jen, turning to walk away.

Rose immediately jumped up to her feet and ran for the toilets. She heard Mrs. Mackenzie calling her name as she reached the corridor but Rose wasn't about to stop.

Rose spent the next hour in the sick room at school. Mrs. Mackenzie seemed to have some idea of what the other kids were saying. Rose wouldn't be able to deny any of it.

Eventually Mrs. Mackenzie and the nurse decided that Rose was suffering from an anxiety attack. They tried to ring Valerie but she wasn't picking up her mobile.

So when Rose mentioned she was seeing a doctor – a psychiatrist – the nurse asked for the details and immediately rang for an appointment. Unfortunately, the earliest one wasn't until the next day – at six in the evening. For the time being, the nurse felt it was best for Rose to go home – maybe take the next day off as well. Things would settle down at school. They always did, she said. Rose didn't believe her but nodded anyway.

The problem was that the whole school knew her secret now – and they also knew a whole lot of other stuff – stuff even Rose didn't know about: like what she'd done and said, like the fact that she'd obviously been drinking and smoking... How could any of it be true? Rose didn't even like the smell of alcohol, never mind the taste. And as for cigarettes...

None of it made any sense.

Rose desperately needed to see Patricia, but would have to wait a whole day. Then it occurred to her that tomorrow was Wednesday. Patricia didn't even work on Wednesday: it was her gardening day. She'd obviously scheduled a special appointment just for Rose. That made her feel better – at least someone cared about her.

But then she also remembered her promise to Sam that she would take Lucy's shift at the restaurant... which she'd have to miss. And this would mean Rose was almost certainly going to lose her job.

Of course, the events of the party were bound to get back to Valerie. In fact, right now Rose could hear the nurse in her office just outside the sick room, speaking to her mother on the phone (despite lowering her voice, Rose kept hearing the nurse say 'Mrs. Azzopardi' – which kind of gave it away). However, while things weren't going to be pretty at home, they would still be better than they were at school. Rose didn't know how she'd ever be able to show her face there again.

"I just spoke with your Mum Rose," said the nurse popping her head into the sick room. "She's coming to pick you up in twenty minutes, okay?"

Rose nodded.

"Do you need anything?"

Rose shook her head.

"You still have your bucket?" asked the nurse,

Rose lifted the red plastic container next to the bed on which she was sitting. She didn't feel sick anymore, so it didn't matter anyway.

"Well you have a lie down and try to get some rest. I'll tell you when your mum gets here."

Rose nodded again.

She was about to go from the fire back into the frying pan. Tomorrow evening couldn't come soon enough.

Rose and Valerie caught a cab home together from the school, both sitting in the back. Valerie was tight-lipped through the entire journey, leaning against the side pillar away from her daughter.

There seemed to be no explanation for why they had taken a taxi either: Rose noticed her mother's car was in the driveway when they got home. At first she thought Valerie might have been drinking, but it was only just after midday. Besides, her mother appeared to be stone-cold sober. Maybe her car had broken down.

As they walked in through the front door, Valerie put her keys on the hallway table but kept walking, saying (without turning back): "I want you to come and take a look at this."

When Rose caught up with her mother, she found her standing in front of Rose's open wardrobe. "Tell me what this is all about," Valerie said, pulling out Rose's new jeans and blouse and throwing both onto the bed.

"Just my clothes…"

"Exactly. So why do they smell of cigarette smoke?" Valerie asked. At her mother's urging, Rose gingerly picked them up with her fingertips and held them near her nose. Yes: they did smell rank. Rose threw them onto the ground, feeling an urgent need to wash her hands.

"I… don't know Mum…"

"And this?" asked her mother, opening her handbag, pulling out something and holding it up. The object was initially silhouetted against the light of the window so Rose couldn't make out what it was. Eventually her eyes adjusted and she saw that it was a slightly crushed cigarette packet (one that displayed ghastly pictures of mouth cancer). "Is it yours?" asked Valerie.

"No… I haven't seen it before. Where did you find it?" Rose's lower lip trembled as she asked this.

"At the bottom of your wardrobe of course. Where did you think? It must have fallen out of a pocket of your jeans. Or maybe you just threw it in there next to your shoes – you tell me."

Abruptly Rose started crying.

Valerie stood quiet for a moment before saying: "You need to stop feeling sorry for yourself and face the consequences of your actions Rose. You need to own your mistakes. You can start by being honest with me."

"I... wish I could tell you what happened Mum," Rose replied between sobs. "But I just... don't know..."

"Where were you last night? It was last night, wasn't it?"

Rose nodded, wiping furiously at her eyes as she tried to compose herself. "I waited... for you to fall asleep, then I went to the Chiongs' party," she said. "The twins had... invited me."

"But I told you that you weren't allowed to go out on Halloween. You deliberately disobeyed me."

Rose, who was still weeping softly with her fists bunched-up in her eyes, managed to whisper: "I'm sorry..."

Valerie sighed. "So what happened? The nurse told me you got into some sort of trouble – that the kids were laughing at you and it made you anxious enough to vomit. The nurse was so worried, she even arranged an appointment with Dr. Clarke. How did it get this bad? I thought you had turned the corner."

Rose shrugged, wiping her eyes and sniffing in spasms.

"Speak to me Rose," said Valerie, holding up the cigarette packet. "When did it start to go wrong? Last night? Or has this being going on for some time?" Without warning, Valerie stepped forward and sniffed her daughter's breath. She did it so suddenly that Rose was startled and flinched back. "Hm. I can't smell anything on you now," Valerie said, almost to herself. "Good Heavens Rose – this just isn't like you at all. Please tell me: what is going on?"

"I… I wish I knew Mum."

"That's not much of an explanation. And I'm not leaving until I get a better one," she said, sitting down on the bed and patting the space next to her for Rose to sit down.

With her body still racked by sobs, Rose eased herself onto the bed next to her mother. Eventually she managed to say: "I… waited for you to go to sleep. It was late – after nine. I heard you snoring, so… I went down to the Chiongs' house. But… people were already leaving and everything seemed to be pretty much… over."

"Did anyone see you?"

"Yes – Mr. and Mrs. Chiong met me at the door. Except they talked to me as if… I'd already been there earlier on in the evening. They seemed…" Rose took a deep series of staggered breaths, and continued: "I don't know – angry. Like I'd done something… bad or embarrassing. You know how strict they are. Except… I hadn't. Not that I could remember anyway…" Rose started crying again and Valerie put her arms around her daughter, letting Rose lean her head against her chest.

"Okay, what about the cigarettes, love? How did they get in your cupboard?" Rose shook her head and burrowed her face into her mother's bosom, sobbing harder still. After a while her mother pulled her away, held her face in her hands and wiped her tears with her thumbs. "You can tell me Rose. I won't be angry anymore."

"That's the... thing... Mum," said Rose between gasps. "I don't remember going to the party early. I thought I was here with you. I couldn't even find what I had planned to wear," she said, pointing to the clothes on the ground. "So I had to grab something else. The next thing I knew... I'd turned up too late: the Chiongs' party had finished. So I came back home. But when I opened my cupboard, I saw my missing clothes were back on their hangers. I didn't even think to smell them. Then I went to school and they said I'd been smoking. And drinking. They said that I... kissed... Jonathan Chiong. Like, I forced myself on him – and really embarrassed myself..."

Valerie studied her daughter's face carefully as she listened, then brought her in for a tight hug.

"You believe me don't you Mum? Please say you believe me," said Rose, speaking into the fabric of her mother's top.

"I do sweetheart," Valerie said softly.

"But what do I do?" asked Rose, her voice muffled against Valerie's shoulder, a wet patch appearing there from her saliva and tears.

"Let's hear what Dr. Clarke has to say tomorrow eh? We'll take it from there."

"I'm so sorry Mum. I'm so sorry…" said Rose, crying again.

"Shh, shh," soothed Valerie. "It's not your fault dear child." Her eyes focused into middle distance and then welled up. "I'm afraid it's mine. All mine."

Some hours later Rose woke up to the grey twilight of the late afternoon. She wondered if her mother was around. Then she heard a chopping sound coming from the kitchen. Soon after the ABC news theme could be heard through the wall. Rose sat up groggily, switched on her bedside light and squinted in the sudden brightness. On the ceiling she could see the 'glow in the dark' stars her father had put up when they'd first moved in – back when she was still a little girl. That seemed a lifetime ago.

The faucet turned on in the kitchen. Moments later she heard the kettle. Then there were more chopping sounds. Meanwhile the microwave pinged. Valerie was making an effort again: she was picking herself up, dusting herself off and starting again. Maybe Rose needed to do the same – owning her mistakes would be the first step.

But how could she do that without being able to remember them?

Impulsively, Rose held her hand up and tried to smell

her breath. Of course, this was useless – she couldn't smell anything at all. Then she remembered a trick Tony had once taught her. He said: "If you want to know how your breath smells, lick your arm and smell that." So she did. Okay, it smelled stale. Pretty awful really: like what you'd expect from someone who'd just been sleeping. But there wasn't even a hint of smoker's breath. How long did cigarettes linger on your breath? She had no idea.

Rose tried to imagine what it would be like to breathe in cigarette smoke. Try as she might, she couldn't even begin to. Surely if she were a smoker, she'd have some residual memory of it? Surely that was one part of your memory you couldn't erase? After all, she might wake up tomorrow and forget ever having eaten strawberries – but she was pretty sure that if someone asked her how a strawberry tasted, she'd still know.

For the first time since Monday, Rose felt more intrigued than afraid: it was a mystery. She was going to think this mystery through until she solved it.

With her heart pounding, Rose reached under the bed and pulled out her pot of money and began counting. She knew from the first count that she was exactly twenty five dollars short. Two more counts simply confirmed this.

Next, Rose grabbed her iPad and looked up 'cigarettes' and 'Australia' and 'cost'. She quickly discovered that a packet typically cost just under twenty five dollars. So Rose had apparently used her own money to buy the cigarettes.

But she also remembered counting her money on Sunday night – and not a cent had been missing then. Which meant that she must have bought the cigarettes on Monday. Except she had been at school the whole day…

Rose needed to try to make sense of it all. What was it Patricia had said? She needed 'cognitive behaviour therapy' – which involved keeping up her journal. Yet she hadn't touched it since their first 'get to meet you' session (not counting the picture of Jon on Halloween).

So Rose reached under the bed, felt around till she found the bound volume she used for recording her most private thoughts, pulled it out and unclipped the pen from the stiff cover. After that, she adjusted her pillows up against the headrest and leaned back. She would write down everything that had happened over the last week – in as much detail as she could remember. She'd do it in the style of a graphic novel: a mystery. Because that is what this was – what she was.

"Well you certainly know how to express yourself through your art Rose," said Patricia, taking off her reading glasses. "I want you to know how honoured I feel that you let me read your journal. I can only imagine how hard it must have been for you to open up like this. I'm proud of you."

Rose simply shrugged. They were seated on chairs around a coffee table near the old fireplace, with Rose leaning forward, her shoulders hunched, one knee pumping up and down again.

"I don't think I would have been able to understand everything that's happened without seeing this. And your artwork is also breathtaking. You're very talented, you know that?"

Rose looked away – out through the window into the grey light.

Patricia put the journal on the coffee table and pushed it gently towards Rose. "I want you to keep up your entries, okay? It's very important."

"So am I going crazy or what?" blurted out Rose.

Patricia shook her head. "We don't use labels like that Rose. They aren't helpful."

"I don't care about labels – I need to know what's happening to me. Even if it's bad."

The doctor leaned in and said softly: "You are going through a difficult time in your life. And sometimes when that happens, your brain chemistry can change a little. We need to put it right. That's all."

"You really think I can be normal again?"

"We don't use the word 'normal' either Rose. No one is 'normal' – we're all different."

"I told you, I don't care what you call it – I just can't live like this: not remembering things... not knowing if I've done something wrong... not knowing if I've humiliated myself..."

"I know it's hard. But we'll get you there. We just need to take it one step at a time. You have to trust me. And, more importantly, you have to trust yourself."

"So what's wrong with me Patricia? Is there a name for it? I thought I just had kleptomania... But now..."

"It's called 'dissociative identity disorder'. Have you heard of it?"

Rose shook her head.

"We used to call it 'multiple personality disorder'. How do I explain it..? Have you seen the film 'Fight Club' – the one with Brad Pitt?"

Rose frowned and said: "No, I don't think so."

"It's based on a book... The movie came out not too long ago – in 1999, I think."

"That was the year before I was born," observed Rose.

Patricia smiled. "Sorry – it still seems like yesterday to me. I guess I'm showing my age. Anyway, the main character in the movie had dissociative identity disorder. In his case, he had two different personalities – just like you."

"You mean, I'm two different people?"

"In a way," replied the doctor. "There's the Rose

that's sitting here now… and then there's another Rose who seems to be rebellious, resentful – angry even. She probably has a right to be after everything that's happened to her. She dresses in black, she smokes, she drinks. Basically, she does all the things she's not supposed to."

"So why can't I remember this… other Rose?"

"I wish I could tell you. My best guess is that your brain puts up a kind of wall – separating your two personalities. The memories of each personality are kept in different parts of your brain; parts that might not mix or share information with each other."

"So I don't remember the other Rose and she doesn't remember me?"

Patricia pondered the question for a while before answering. "It's hard to say at this point. She might know all about you but you might not know anything about her. Or you might both be living in completely different worlds – where you only learn about each other when one of you gets into trouble."

"But I've always known when I was in trouble…"

"You mean, like when you were caught stealing?" suggested Patricia.

"Yes."

"Well maybe you were aware that you were doing something wrong, but the other Rose wasn't. Maybe the shoe is now on the other foot: you're aware of something that she's done wrong."

"Is she getting me back then?"

"No, Rose, I'm just using an analogy. Remember: there aren't really two people. This is all happening inside you. It's not real."

"So then I am going crazy," Rose said, her eyes welling up.

"No – I didn't say that."

"You said it's not real…"

"Well Rose, in a way nothing we experience inside is 'real': everything we see, hear, feel, smell – all of it – gets to us second-hand. What we experience is a kind of recording that happens a fraction of a second after 'reality'. Think of it as a YouTube video. You watch YouTube videos, right?"

Rose nodded, wiping away a stray tear.

"You know how sometimes the internet is slow, and the video 'buffers' – pauses as it is loading? Well our brains also have a kind of 'buffer'. You can think of our eyes as a kind of camera lens that lets our brain record a video. That video is then buffered. We get to see it later – only a millisecond later, but later nonetheless. It happens so fast we usually don't notice the difference between the real world and the video. But there is a difference."

"You mean we sometimes notice the difference?"

"Sure. Have you ever been doing something new –

like visiting somewhere you've never been or speaking to a stranger – and suddenly you feel like you've done it before?"

"Yes – I get that all the time."

"It's called *déjà vu* – it's French for 'already seen'. Some people think this is what happens when your brain gets a bit mixed up – and you notice that 'buffer' we've been talking about."

"So the girl in the attic…" began Rose.

"Is you. Your brain is mixing up signals. In this case you're remembering things that might have happened to you – maybe while you were living in the attic, or maybe while you were the 'other Rose'. Basically, you can think of it as a long buffer."

"What about the picture of Jon in my journal?"

"It's yours. I'm sure you can recognise your own style, right? Except that you – this Rose sitting here with me today – didn't get to see that particular 'YouTube video', so you don't remember drawing it."

Rose looked down, shaking her head slowly. "I don't know. It just doesn't make sense. I mean, I remember being at home during the party – waiting for my mother to go to sleep…"

"Or is that just a memory you've constructed to fill a gap? Your brain hates gaps – it'll do anything to fill them."

"Okay then – what about the cigarettes? The only

time I could have bought them was on Monday. But I was at school all day!"

"Are you sure you didn't pass a newsagent or deli on the way to your bus?"

"No! Well… I suppose I might have…"

"Don't you think it's possible that the 'other you' went in and bought the cigarettes?"

"I suppose…" Rose ventured, staring out of the window. Eventually she asked: "So why is it happening to me? Why now?"

"I'm afraid no one really understands why people get dissociative identity disorder. But if I were to guess, I'd say you're suffering from depression and anxiety – because of everything that has happened to you: your parents breaking up, your mother's drinking, your banishment to the attic… I think you tried to cope by doing compulsive things – like washing your hands or locking the door three times or counting your money. It was your way of feeling like you had some control of your world. Stealing became part of that. Except that stealing also got you into trouble. So now, your brain might be coping with everything by separating your memories to protect you – almost as if you were two different people."

The room went silent. Once again, it was beginning to get dark – so dark Rose could no longer make out Patricia's features. Eventually her doctor got up and walked to her mahogany desk. She was nothing more than a blur: a moving shadow in the room.

"So how can we fix it?" asked Rose.

"Well… we can treat it," said Patricia switching on her desk light and opening up her top drawer. "There are medications I can give you. No one really knows which one is going to work best for a particular patient: everyone responds differently. But in your case, I want to prescribe a mild anti-depressant. It should help you sleep and stop your anxiety attacks." She rifled around until she found a prescription pad. "The rest of the treatment is the same as before: I want you to keep writing and drawing in your journal – as often as possible." She began to scribble on the sheet and a few seconds later she ripped it off and gave it to Rose. "Take one tablet just before bed. Let's give that a try, eh?" She looked at her watch. "I'll see you same time next week – how about that?"

"Okay…" said Rose, holding the script and wondering how anyone could possibly read the handwriting.

"In the meantime," said Patricia, "if you get worried about anything – anything at all – just call me. Here's my mobile number." She scribbled furiously on another notepad, tore off the top sheet off and handed it to Rose.

A few minutes later, Rose was standing out in the fresh sea breeze next to her bicycle, combing the strands of hair from her face before she put on her helmet. The sun had gone down and the streetlights had come on.

A warm smell of garlic came wafting from the restaurant across the road and made Rose think about her job. She had called the day before to cancel her shift, saying she had a medical appointment. Sofia hadn't sounded happy. No doubt Rose would find out on Friday if she had been fired. She wasn't going to worry about it until then.

Truth

Rose walked into the dining room to find her mother at the table, a plate of half-finished food in front of her, staring at a full glass of red wine that she was holding by the stem with both hands. "I saved you some dinner. You'll have to warm it up," Valerie said without turning around.

"Okay – thanks. Smells wonderful. What did you make?"

"A stir-fry," Valerie replied absently, still holding onto the glass, her eyes focused somewhere into middle distance.

"Are you okay Mum?"

"Me? Yes – fine," said Valerie turning to face her daughter. "Say – how did it go with Dr. Clarke?"

"It seems I've got something called 'dissociative identity disorder'. Patricia's put me on some anti-depressants." Rose handed her mother the script and Valerie frowned as she donned the reading glasses hanging around her neck.

"Isn't that where you have multiple personalities?"

"Something like that."

"That sounds serious Rose…"

"Nah. Patricia said it was most likely just a temporary thing. Just my way of dealing with stress. I'll be okay once the meds kick in after a couple of days."

"Hm. I hope she knows what she's doing…"

"Don't worry Mum – I trust her. By the way, she's given me the rest of the week off school."

"Good. The last thing you needed was more harassment from the kids in your class," Valerie said, handing back the script and removing her glasses.

Rose was about to walk out when something made her reconsider. Her mother had resumed her unfocused staring. She'd recently lost weight from her already slight frame, so that she was now almost bird-like in appearance, with the vertebra of her upper back and neck protruding as she hunched forward while her bony arms and hands once again stretched out to clutch at the stem of the wineglass. Rose pulled up a chair and sat down next to her mother.

Valerie's eyes stayed unfocused as she said: "The stress that's caused your condition… That would be because of me."

"No Mum. Patricia said it was a whole lot of stuff: me stealing, Dad leaving us…"

"Your Dad didn't leave us Rose. I kicked him out."

"What do you mean? I was there. I remember the

argument…"

"You heard the tail-end of an argument. What you didn't hear was that we'd been arguing since the previous night when I told him I wanted him out of the house. Forever. Your father wanted to stay. In fact, he begged me to let him. But I told him it was over."

"Why? Because of his gambling?"

Valerie nodded, turning the glass around so that the wine sloshed a little up the sides. "Your father started crying – the first time I'd ever seen him do that. He promised he was about to make a fortune so none of us would ever have to work again. He said he'd worked it all out. He had this 'system' – his 'cosmic formula'…"

"I remember," Rose replied. "I used to believe in it."

"You know what? So did I," admitted Valerie. "Your father could be pretty convincing. Especially when he started winning like he did for that short time. Remember? It was just after he put up that damned wall in the attic. He actually won the Melbourne Cup – quite a bit of money. He would have won even more, except I would only let him put a few hundred on the race. In the end, he had the first, second, third and fourth places all pegged. Fiorente in first, Red Cadeaux in second…"

"Mount Athos in third, Simenon in fourth," finished Rose. "How can I forget?"

"But it didn't last did it?" said Valerie with a sigh. Abruptly, she laughed. "The French call it *folie à deux* –

the madness of two. He sucked me right in for a while: into his world of magic – of 'cosmic formulae'."

Rose smiled: this was her second French lesson in one day. "Better make that *folie à trois* Mum – I believed him as well, remember?"

Valerie nodded, let go of the wine glass, turned to her daughter and took her hands. "I don't know what happened to him Rosie. I mean, he used to place bets on the horses when you were little but it was just a kind of hobby. He seemed to have it under control. Then he suddenly became obsessive. In the end I couldn't take it anymore. He became a different man – and it happened almost overnight. I remember he even started smelling different. I don't know how to describe it: a smell of desperation – stress hormones or something…"

"I remember that smell," replied Rose, "even when he was painting that stupid wall."

"It took a toll on him, physically: he aged so quickly," said Valerie absently.

"Yes – his hair went grey," recalled Rose.

Valerie let go of her daughter's hands and slouched back in her chair, sighing deeply. "Of course, he stopped talking to me – about anything. All he wanted to do was look at those damned race lists online and check them against his notebook. Oh, at first he tried to pretend everything was okay. We both did. But in the end, it was clear that I couldn't reach him anymore. Even he stopped pretending. Remember how he moved up into the attic? We stayed like that for a while. Then one day I told him we were finished: that he had to go. So as you can see Rose, your father didn't leave us – I kicked him out."

"Well you had to do it Mum. It's not as if you had a choice. We couldn't live like that any longer, could we? Even I told Dad I'd had enough."

Valerie raised her eyebrows. "When?"

"The day he left. We were up in the attic. I called him a loser. I said I was ashamed of him. Those were the last words I ever said to him..."

"Oh sweetheart... Come here," Valerie said, putting her arm around her daughter. Rose leaned in and placed her head against her mother's chest, listening to the familiar dull thumping of her heart.

"Don't you see? My condition isn't your fault," Rose said after a while.

"Ah, but I'm afraid it is," replied Valerie. "It's my fault because I'm the one who drinks."

"That's just the way you're trying to cope. We're all doing the best we can."

Valerie inhaled deeply. Then she pulled her daughter away from her, holding her by the shoulders and looking into her eyes. "It's time I told you the truth. I've been sitting here for some time, trying to summon up the courage."

"What is it? You're getting me worried," said Rose.

"I'm not working at the law firm any more. They fired me a couple of weeks ago. Well, they don't call it that exactly – they say they gave me a 'redundancy package'."

"Why? Why would they fire you?"

"Turning up late and being hung-over pretty much every day would have had something to do with it. Making mistakes more and more often would also have played a role. I suppose the final straw was getting drunk one too many times at Friday drinks… It's not exactly a good look – especially in a firm that's losing clients and is wanting to shed staff. I guess I became an obvious target."

"But you've been going to work every day!"

"No Rose. I've been pretending to. I've been leaving in the mornings, then coming back once you were safely in school. I used to go out again in the afternoon – usually to a pub – and come home in the evening."

"Why Mum? Why did you do it?"

"I was ashamed. I guess I was hoping to get another job and smooth everything over before you found out."

Rose suddenly remembered what she'd almost said to Lane outside the court: *Tell her yourself – you work in the same firm.*

"There's more," said Valerie. "On Monday the police pulled me over in the car. I got booked for drink-driving. I've lost my licence Rose. I'll have to pay a fine as

few days might leave you feeling odd. Just put up with it and it'll get better. You'll see," Patricia had said.

Except that Rose wasn't confident that she could go through any more days like this. An hour after getting up, she was still stumbling about, walking into walls and dozing whenever she sat down for more than a few minutes.

She was at the breakfast nook, propping her chin up on one hand, trying to stay awake. Valerie seemed to materialise out of nowhere and, with shaky hands, put something in front of her. As Rose's eyes gradually brought it into focus, she saw that it was an open plastic storage container in which there was a pastrami sandwich on dark rye bread, cut in half and bursting with avocado, spinach and alfalfa.

"Thanks Mum but I don't know if I can eat just yet."

"It's your lunch silly. You've got to keep up your strength," replied Valerie, kissing her daughter on the forehead. Rose could smell make-up and perfume. When she leaned back she saw that her mother was in her business suit.

"Where are you going?"

"To court for my drink-driving charge. I'll be pleading guilty – so one way or another, I hope to get it over and done with today. I'm taking the bus into town, so don't expect me till much later, okay?"

"How much later?"

"Well… I have some interviews lined up in town after the hearing – one at two o'clock and another at four – so I probably won't be back before you head off to work."

"Interviews? Do you mean for jobs?" asked Rose.

Valerie nodded and drained a cup of coffee.

"When did you organise that?"

"You have to remember Rose: I got fired ages ago. And I wasn't lying last Friday when I told you that I was planning to turn my life around. In fact, at that stage I'd already sent off half a dozen applications. I decided not to say anything because I didn't want to get your hopes up. Anyway, as luck would have it, two firms got back to me yesterday. It seems they both need a specialist in Family Law – urgently."

"Wow Mum… How do you feel about it – I mean, having interviews today, of all days?" asked Rose, swaying slightly on her stool.

"I'd feel a whole lot better if I wasn't about to face court on a drink-driving charge. I'd also feel a lot better if I wasn't in the middle of 'drying out' from alcohol. But that's life – isn't it?" said Valerie with a sigh. "You don't always get what you want. You just have to make the best of what you get. Anyway, I'd better be off or I'll miss my bus," said her mother, giving Rose another quick kiss and a hug. "Wish me luck," she said as she headed out into the corridor.

"Good luck Mum. Knock 'em dead."

Valerie paused, held up crossed fingers and smiled, then disappeared through the door.

By late afternoon Rose started to feel better. She could see herself managing the walk up to the restaurant (where earlier on it had seemed almost impossible). If anything, Rose was feeling sicker at the thought of dealing with Sam and Sofia than she was from the anti-depressant. It wasn't exactly an ideal time for her to be begging to keep her job. But if her mother could put her best foot forward today, so could she.

Besides, she'd already started the whole business of turning her life around and there was no point stopping now. In particular, Rose was thinking about how she'd gone to the pharmacy the previous day to get her script – and apologise to the staff for stealing.

At first the assistant behind the desk hadn't recognised her. "Can I help you?" she asked with a smile.

"Um… I have a script," Rose said, proffering the piece of paper.

"Do we have your Medicare details?"

"Yes… my mum and I come here a lot…"

It was at that point that the pharmacist on the raised platform behind looked up from the work she was doing and recognised Rose. The assistant shared the same moment of realisation: Rose could tell from her widened eyes and the fact that she had stepped back.

"I.. also wanted to speak with you guys. To say how sorry I am. About everything." Rose was conscious of the other patrons in the pharmacy who were obviously listening in. One of them had pushed a fully-laden trolley up from the supermarket and was standing right behind her, her face twisted into a scowl. Another older man was sitting waiting for his script to be filled, tapping his crutch on the carpeted ground and twisting his jaw from side to side like a cow chewing cud.

"The pharmacist will be with you in a moment," said the assistant hesitantly, handing Rose's script up and retreating sideways – like a crab – to deal with the grouchy trolley-woman.

Eventually the pharmacist came down. "Mr. Arnaud?" she called. The man with the crutch raised himself awkwardly and swivelled his way to the counter. It seemed to take forever for him to sign the script with a spidery signature, take out the wallet that was pushed tightly down the front pocket of his trousers and finally extract the exact amount of money.

When the transaction was complete, the man grabbed his paper bag of medicines and hobbled off, leaving Rose face-to-face with the same pharmacist who had caught her stealing. The name badge said "Winnie". Rose had always known her to be friendly and accommodating. But right now she was standing stiffly with her hands at her sides, her lips pursed, a frown creasing her forehead. Her assistant looked pretty much the same.

"I... I'm glad you're both here. Because I wanted to apologise to you. I don't know why I did it... the stealing. I've seen a doctor and she says I'm... not well. I know it's not an excuse. I just wanted to say how sorry I was. And that I'm seeing someone to make sure it doesn't happen again." Rose gestured to the script which the pharmacist was holding. She looked down, read it, then nodded slowly.

"It's not every day we get someone coming in and apologising like this. I think you're being very brave," said Winnie. "Thank you. I'll fix this," she said, waving the script. "It'll only a take minute." Both Winnie and her assistant smiled.

Rose looked up at that moment and caught sight of Nathan's sister at a checkout in the adjacent supermarket. She was staring, her mouth agape.

So Rose could finally go to her local pharmacy again: she certainly no longer had to hide her face as she passed it on the way to Valentino's – two doors down in the same centre.

Which was where Rose was headed now: to face the music with Sam. Or Sofia. Maybe both.

The restaurant door jingled as Rose walked in. The

evening bookings would be arriving soon and the chairs had to be taken down, the tables set, the specials board re-written… the usual routine. The question was: would Sam let her get on with it and fire her at the end of the shift – or would he tell her to get out straight away?

Rose saw Giacomo – the pizza oven guy – and he gave her a wave and a smile (Rose always wondered if he had a crush on her but he was so shy it was hard to tell). Then Matteo, the maître d', came out from the kitchen whistling. He barely paused as he passed by, giving Rose a friendly wink. So far, so good.

"Ah, there you are," said a voice from behind her. Rose turned to see Sam pushing his way between the tables, his shirt catching on the upturned chairs. "Get dressed will you, and start getting this place ready. What am I paying you for?"

Rose nodded and started for the toilets.

"And Rose," called Sam.

Rose stopped at the door which she had pushed half-open. "Yes Sam?"

Her boss walked up closer. "Thanks for coming in on Wednesday. I know you had a medical appointment and I'm sorry you had to cancel it. But thank God you did because, seriously, we would have been totally stuffed without you – especially with Matteo away. I tell you, I was ready to pack in this blasted business. So when you turned up… Let's just say I've never been happier to see you. And you did good, by the way."

Rose puzzled over this, her frown accentuated by the fluorescent light coming from inside the toilets. Wednesday? In the end, all Rose could say was: "Sure Sam."

"One more thing," he added, just as she was about to go through the door again. Sam lowered his voice. "Please – if you want to take a smoke, do what Matteo does eh? Go up to the south side where the bins are. Customers are coming and going to the carpark all the time. It's not a good look for staff to be seen having a puff out there. Capisci?"

Rose nodded.

Unfortunately it turned out that Rose hadn't yet finished 'running the gauntlet': she still had Sofia to go.

"Look what the cat dragged in," she said as Rose came out of the toilets, tying her apron. Sofia was at the till and checking the list of bookings in the diary against the table numbers. "At least you've gotten rid of that horrid make-up. Did your mother make you scrub your face? I would have."

"I don't know what you're talking about," said Rose.

"The Goth thing. Who does that now? Black lipstick, pale foundation? Seriously? We were desperate on Wednesday so I let it go, but don't you dare come to work looking like that again."

Rose decided not to respond. Her 'other self' had obviously come to work – somehow. To save the day, maybe? Who knew? And how did she manage it? Rose distinctly remembered her long session with Patricia, then riding home on her bike in the dark, then speaking with Valerie at the dinner table until late… That had all happened on Wednesday night. How could she have been working at the same time? Were her memories just 'gaps' filled in by her brain? It didn't feel like it. None of it made sense. But then again, mental illness didn't make sense. Besides, her mind had just been scrambled by anti-depressants.

"Are you just going to stand there staring like a loony? Get moving! Table nine will be here in five minutes!" yelled Sofia. Rose started pulling the chairs off the tables and went behind the bar where the folded chequered tablecloths were stored. "You know, I don't care that Sam is suddenly singing your praises," said Sofia. "He wasn't there when you spoke to me so rudely. If it had been up to me, I'd have fired you," she said, snorting. Rose was conscious that Sofia continued to stare at her as she set out the plates, cutlery and the swan-folded napkins. "By the way, you sure had some nerve asking for cash on Wednesday night. Especially after that speech you gave me about wanting to be paid 'properly'. I don't know what made you think we'd go back to 'business as usual'. And what is it with you and your damned $19.00 an hour?" Rose heard Sofia snort again and turned around in time to catch her shaking her head. "Sam won't listen to me now: he says I'm making it up – or imagining it. Can you believe that? He's taking your side! Well I've got your measure Missy – don't forget that. Six hours at $17.70 is $106.20 – and like I said on Wednesday, that's all you're getting. Check your account – I've already transferred it."

Rose just nodded. Then, to Sofia's amazement, she simply said: "Thanks Sofia."

"You seem a bit subdued tonight," noted Evan. "On Wednesday you were really on fire. Heck, I think I saw you carry seven plates at once. When did you learn to do that?" They were in the corridor next to the kitchen, leaning against the walls, waiting for the last of the stragglers to leave. Rose felt exhausted – more so than usual: the anti-depressant was still affecting her. She couldn't bear to think she'd have to take another one when she got home.

"Yeah well – I've got a bit of a… chest thingy…" Rose affected a cough for emphasis. As she did so, the sound reminded her of the girl in the attic.

"Smoking won't help that," ventured Evan.

"Mind your own business," snapped Rose, but Evan just laughed, tilting his head back.

"You're a funny creature, you know that?" he said,

still chuckling.

"What do you mean?"

"Oh, I don't know. It's just that I can't work you out. On Wednesday you were…"

"A Goth. I know. Why can't people be who they want to be? What's with all the judgment?"

"I promise, I'm not judging you – at all. Just my natural curiosity."

"You know what curiosity did to the cat, don't you?" shot back Rose. She was quoting one of her mother's favourite lines.

"I do actually – as you probably remember from our conversation at around this time on Wednesday night."

"Eh? Remind me," said Rose frowning. Here was where she might get into trouble: before the conversation went any further, she'd have to fish for as much information as possible.

"That story I told you – about the cat that got brought in last week. The one that had to be put down, remember?"

"Oh yeah. That one…" Rose didn't have a clue what he was talking about. Had someone brought a cat into Valentino's? Or did they bring cats into WAAPA? If so, what for?

"It happens with the dogs as well of course. They can get themselves into trouble. But at the shelter we don't tend to see those sorts of cases. We get the more tragic ones — you know? Neglect, deliberate injury, abandonment."

"Abandonment?" asked Rose. She was still fishing.

"Yeah. It happens a lot. More than you'd think. People just drive along the Great Eastern Highway and dump animals. The cats go feral, but dogs... they don't cope so well. They don't have a clue really. After all, we're talking family pets here – not wolves. So when we get them, they're usually severely dehydrated. We had this one Great Dane a few months ago who'd run into the bush. We kept getting reported sightings – some as far away as Chidlow – but we couldn't track him down. By the time we caught up with him, he was just skin and bone: he could barely move."

"Um... Where was your... place... again?"

"The shelter's not mine, of course. I just volunteer. It's up in Kalamunda – remember? I started tagging along with my sister who's a vet. But I told you all this last time."

"Oh yeah. Sorry – I'm a bit out of it. The chest... thingy." Rose coughed again.

"Don't kill me, but I really do think you should give up the smoking," said Evan.

Rose clenched her teeth, gave him a sideways scowl but said nothing. Evan laughed again.

"Jokes aside, are you still up for it?"

"For what?"

"The visit. You said on Wednesday you'd like to visit."

"Oh... yeah. Sure."

"Well I'm going there tomorrow, as you know," said Evan. He paused for a moment, looking down at his feet. "I... I could give you a lift, if you wanted. I mean, I live just around the corner. Well, it's not actually around the corner of course, but Mount Lawley isn't exactly far from Mount Hawthorn. If you know what I mean."

Rose's mind was racing ahead, thinking: Patricia had said she should get a pet. Maybe this was her chance. She would look for a dog: a big one – one that could keep her safe... She'd keep it in her bedroom. Maybe she'd get a German Shepherd or American Pit Bull... Something like that.

"Well – how about it?" asked Evan, and Rose realised she'd been staring off into space again.

"Um... what time?"

"Bright and early, I'm afraid. Like, we'd have to leave no later than 7:30 a.m."

"Um... That's early..."

"For Goths, yeah – I bet," Evan said laughing.

Rose pushed him on the shoulder and frowned, but couldn't help breaking into a grin. She paused before saying: "I don't know – it might be a bit hard for me..."

"To get out of your coffin at that time?"

"Stop it!"

Evan laughed even harder. Sam walked into the corridor and scowled, so Evan stifled himself, nodding to Sam in apology.

"Okay… I'll do it," Rose blurted out as soon as Sam had left.

Abruptly Evan nudged her with his elbow and pointed into the dining lounge saying: "Hey – it looks like your table is all done. Lucky you – my people seem to want to hang around." Rose followed the line of his finger and saw her customers getting up, dusting themselves off, so she headed to the till. "Catch you tomorrow then," said Evan as she walked away. "Remember: bright and early. Hope you can stand sunlight!" He was laughing again.

"You did what?" exclaimed Valerie.

"I said I'd go along. It's an animal shelter Mum."

"After everything you've been through, you want to talk about pets? You really are going crazy!"

"That's not nice," murmured Rose.

"You're right – I'm sorry. Look, it's late. Why don't we talk about this in the morning."

"Because he's coming here at 7:30 a.m."

"Rose! How could you?"

"Patricia told me it was a good idea!"

"And how are we going to afford it – eh?"

"It's a shelter Mum… You don't buy the dogs, you

adopt them."

Valerie scoffed. "You have to pay for de-sexing, microchipping and a whole bunch of other stuff. It'll cost at least a couple of hundred dollars – probably more!"

"Well I'll pay – I have enough."

"Oh Rose… Just when I think the dust has settled, you come up with something else. Honestly, sometimes I just don't understand you."

"Please Mum…"

"Okay – leave aside what Patricia said and tell me this: why do you want a dog? Why now?"

"Because… I want to feel safe…"

"Safe? Are you kidding me?"

"No – I told you that I keep hearing the girl… the one up there," Rose said, pointing at the ceiling. "I heard her just last night, even as I was falling asleep, all groggy from the anti-depressant."

"But you know she isn't real Rose!"

"Yeah, I know. But that doesn't mean I don't feel scared. All the time."

"How is a dog going to help?"

"I'll get a big one," Rose said. "The dog can stay in my room and I'll know that I'm not alone."

"A big dog costs more to feed…" said Valerie, running her hands through her thin hair to pull it back into a ponytail. Rose noticed that her hands weren't shaking quite so much.

"Like I said – I'll pay."

"Typical teenager: you think your money can stretch as far as the horizon. Well I'm sorry to break it to you darling but it can't."

There was silence after that. Rose knew that her mother was right. So they stood there in the kitchen, Valerie with one hand holding her chin, deep in thought as if calculating, and Rose holding her backpack by one strap as it lay on the floor. Abruptly Valerie said: "So who is this guy anyway?"

"Just Evan – from work. You met him once when he dropped me off."

"The uni guy? I think he likes you."

"No Mum – don't be gross. He's just a friend."

"What's gross about it? He's cute."

"Mum – hearing you say that is even more gross."

"Be that as it may, you can't go… not on your own anyway. There's no way I'm about to let my daughter go driving off into the hills with some… some uni student actor-fellow who might be an axe-murderer, as far as I know – and who should be chasing girls his own age. Besides, if we're getting a dog, I'm going to help choose it."

"Does that mean we're going?" Rose let go of her backpack and clapped her hands together.

"Yes, I suppose it does," said Valerie sighing. She was

immediately overwhelmed by her daughter's tight hug.

Rose pulled away a second later, still holding her mother's elbows: "Wait, I forgot to ask: how did it go today?"

Valerie smiled. "I got off lightly because I was only just over the limit. Also it was a first offence and all that. So the judge gave me a three month licence suspension and a five hundred dollar fine."

"Whew – that's a relief! And what about the job interviews?"

Valerie's face broke into a wider grin. "They went well sweetheart. Really well." She caught another fierce hug around the neck and broke into laughter. "Steady on Rosie," she said somewhat breathlessly as her daughter squeezed the air out of her lungs. "Let's not count our chickens just yet. Now how about we get to bed, eh? We'll need all the sleep we can get if we're to get up so damned early."

Rose sat on the stained IKEA circular rug in the middle of the bedroom, her pot of money in front of her, the single twenty five watt globe above her casting long shadows around the room.

She was exactly $106.00 short. She knew because she'd counted her money three times. Then she'd checked all the pockets of her clothes, her drawers... everywhere. The money was gone. The other Rose must have taken it. But why?

She suddenly had a thought: Rose reached under the bed, grabbed her journal and flipped to the last page as quickly as she could, feeling her pulse quicken as she did so.

There was a fresh entry. It comprised a picture of two fifty dollar notes with wings on them. The other Rose had done a pretty good job of drawing Edith Cowan and David Unaipon whose portraits appear on either side of the Australian fifty dollar note (Rose knew both of them from her history studies). Below that, there was a message, in Rose's own handwriting. It said:

> *'Read your graphic novella. It's pretty cool, you know? Sorry about the mess I got you into. I didn't want you to lose your job. But I'm not working for free either. Anyway, I couldn't find twenty cents, so you can keep that.'*

Rose put the journal down, picked up the box of anti-depressants lying next to her on the rug and opened it up. She could see the tablets still in their blister packaging and the gap left from the one she'd taken the previous night, its torn foil folded to one side, the plastic crushed.

Then she closed the lid and pushed the box, her journal and her pot of money under the bed.

Grow

"You look remarkably... awake. I thought you'd be all dozy again this morning from your medication. I'm afraid I didn't think about that at all last night when we were talking. Are you going to be okay travelling up to the shelter?" asked Valerie opening the fridge door.

Rose, who was sitting at the breakfast nook chewing a spoonful of Weetbix, covered her mouth as she replied: "Yeah, I'll be fine."

Valerie frowned and looked into the fridge. Rose heard her say: "Boy – you sure got used to those anti-depressants quickly." Then her mother suddenly peered around the door, raising an eyebrow. "Or did you?"

Rose pretended she couldn't speak because her mouth was full mouth and waved her hand in a circle.

"You didn't take your tablet last night – did you?" said Valerie eventually.

"No Mum... I didn't," admitted Rose.

"Why the hell not? Was it because of this boy?"

"His name is Evan, Mum. And no, it had nothing to do with him, so please stop saying that. I just completely forgot about my meds when I agreed to go to the shelter. I remembered just before I went to bed – but I didn't want to be all spaced-out today, especially in the morning. And it was late anyway."

"Oh well – missing one dose shouldn't matter. You'll just have to take one tonight. You realise you'll be starting from scratch again?"

Rose nodded.

"Hang on a minute…" said Valerie as she shut the fridge door. "Rose…"

"What Mum?"

"Look at me. You're thinking of stopping them, aren't you?"

Rose didn't reply

"But you've only tried it once!" said Valerie with a gasp.

"I'll see how I feel tonight, okay," Rose replied. "I'll decide then."

"You will most certainly not! Your doctor gave you that medication and you're going to take it – do you understand me?"

"Mum, it's not that simple."

"Oh yes it is! And I don't want to hear another word about it. For crying out loud, don't you want to get better?"

"I am better."

"Rose Sabina Azzopardi! You do not get better after

taking one tablet!"

"Maybe I was never ill."

"Please tell me you're joking!"

"Mum, last night the people at Valentino's said I'd worked the Wednesday shift this week. And we both know I didn't."

"Oh boy… are we back to that again? Do you think someone is impersonating you at your restaurant? Rose, you have to accept that this is just part of your illness. There is no 'girl in the attic'! She isn't going to parties pretending to be you and she sure as hell isn't going to work for you either!"

"Then how come she worked for me on Wednesday night?"

"I think you're just confused Rose."

"No, I 'm not confused. They told me yesterday that I'd come into work on Wednesday."

"You don't even work on Wednesdays!" shouted Valerie.

"Well normally I don't. But Sam asked me to do it just this once because Lucy was away."

"When did he ask you?"

"A while back. Two weeks ago, I think. I had to say yes. He was going to fire me if I didn't."

"Well I'm sorry Rose, but that never happened… You have to trust me – it never happened!"

"Yes, it did!" Rose yelled back. "I didn't want to tell

you about it before because I knew you'd just get angry about me working on a school night. In the end it didn't matter because I had to cancel in order to go to my appointment with Patricia. Then, when I went to work last night, Sam thanked me for turning up on Wednesday. Even Sofia said I'd been there."

"Oh honey – you have to know this is all in your mind."

"What's in my mind Mum? Did I imagine my appointment with Patricia? Did I imagine that we talked about you being fired – and how you got busted by the cops for drinking and driving?"

Rose realised that both she and her mother were getting louder and louder.

"No, of course you didn't imagine any of that. But honey, trust me: no one told you that you were working on Wednesday – that bit all came from your mind!"

"Mum, they told me just last night! I remember it as clear as day!"

"Yes, I know. And last night you were still heavily affected by your anti-depressant medication. You remember that don't you?"

"Oh, I remember alright. I also remember Sam thanking me for 'cancelling my medical appointment'. I remember Sofia telling me off for looking like a Goth. I remember Sam telling me off for smoking in the car park – saying that I should do it near the bins like Matteo does!"

"If they said anything like that, they must have been talking about some other shift."

"No they weren't!" screamed Rose. "They were talking about Wednesday – this last Wednesday the second of November!"

Valerie scoffed. "Oh you are impossible! Listen to yourself Rose – just listen!"

"Well you can ask Evan!"

"I will most certainly not! This is our private business. I am not talking to some… strange young man… about my daughter's mental illness!" Valerie screamed back.

Rose didn't know how to respond. And, in the awkward silence that followed, she and Valerie suddenly became aware of a banging at the front door. They looked at each other, mouths agape. The banging got louder and Valerie started for the door, only to find her daughter pushing ahead of her.

When Rose finally opened it, she saw Evan standing behind the fly-screen with his hands in his jean pockets, wearing a long-sleeved grey work shirt emblazoned with a logo that read "Kalamunda Wildlife Shelter".

"Um. Hi Evan. Sorry – we were in the kitchen and didn't hear you."

"I could tell…" he said, twisting one side of his mouth into a faint smile. He walked in hesitantly, stopping to wipe his feet on the doormat. "I'm really sorry about banging so hard, but I had been knocking at the door for quite a while. And I hate to rush you Rose – but we're running late…"

Rose looked up at the clock in the hall – a 1970s piece that had come with the house, complete with psychedelic letters on a background that had originally been burnt orange but had faded to beige. It read 7:38 a.m.

"Oh – I'm sorry. I'll just grab my things – I won't be a sec," Rose said, feeling the heat radiating from her cheeks. When she looked up she could see her mother standing in the corridor, the pale skin of her neck also patterned with the blotchy redness of a blush. "You remember my mum, don't you? Mum, this is Evan. Evan, Mum."

Valerie extended her hand.

"Hi Mrs. Azzopardi. We met a few months ago," said Evan, leaning forward to shake her hand.

"Please call me Valerie."

"Okay… Valerie. I hope… it's okay for Rose to come along this morning. She said she wanted to… see how the shelter worked."

"She obviously didn't tell you that she wanted to adopt a pet as well," replied Valerie.

"No, actually – she didn't. But if she sees an animal that she likes… we can sort it out at the end of our volunteer work. We knock off at 1:00 p.m."

"Volunteer work eh?" Valerie looked sideways at

Rose who was bent over her backpack, stuffing a jumper in next to her water bottle. "Well it's the shelter's lucky day – you've got another volunteer."

"Eh, who?" asked Evan, eyes wide and scanning from Rose to Valerie and back.

"Me," said Valerie. "I'm coming along."

"Oh… okay then. That should be fine. I didn't realise you were interested in animals…"

"I didn't realise my daughter was either," replied Valerie, grabbing her jacket off the coat rack. "But you learn something new every day."

"Time to wind up," said Evan looking into the kennel. Rose looked over her shoulder. She was using a squeegee to dry the surface. She'd already emptied everything out of the kennel (including a cowering collie, with feet that seemed to stick to the floor), picked up the poops (some of which were still steaming and most of which were stained red – presumably with blood), sprayed disinfectant (everywhere), wire brushed the floors and walls (to get rid of the bits of poop that wouldn't come off any other way) and, finally, hosed everything down. Rose looked down at her good jeans and saw that they were covered in a mix of reddish faecal matter, dirty water and long, matted dog hair. Evan remarked: "You and your mum didn't really dress for the occasion."

"You noticed."

Evan laughed. "I bet you thought it would be all dog walking!"

"Um... something like that," replied Rose.

"I tell you what though – you've both put your backs into it today. We got a lot done. Your mum seems to have enjoyed herself too. She's out there talking to Angela right now. I think I heard her say she wants to come back some time."

Rose stifled a laugh, covering her mouth.

"What's funny?" said Evan, clinging to the wire.

Rose pointed. "I missed a bit of poop on the cage door. It must have got there from the dog's paws. Anyway, you're..." And she laughed out loud as Evan suddenly retracted his hand, looked at it and took out a tissue to wipe the blob off his hand.

"Nervous dog. Must have had gut problems," he said smiling. "You get used to it." Then he laughed too.

"So Rose," said Angela, the shelter manager, "your mother tells me you're interested in adopting a pet?"

She, Angela, Valerie and Evan were walking back to the main centre after cleaning themselves up – as best they could anyway.

Rose nodded. "A dog."

"What kind?"

"I was thinking of a big dog," she said.

"Have you ever owned one before?"

"No. Not even a small one," Rose replied.

"We always wanted to get a dog… but somehow we never got around to it," added Valerie.

"Hm. Well you've seen some of the medium to large dogs we have here. Most are working breeds – the husky, the kelpie cross and the border collie, for example. Then there's the playful breeds that are always full of beans – like that pair of boxers you saw. They all require a lot of exercise and stimulation. Do you think you'll be able to provide that?"

"How often would I need to walk them?" asked Rose.

Angela laughed. "How long is a piece of string? That pair of boxers got dumped probably because they wanted to run all day. I suspect they ended up digging up the whole backyard out of frustration and the owner couldn't take it anymore. We had someone fostering the kelpie cross you took for a walk, but he kept pulling the washing down from the line and tearing it to shreds. He swallowed a whole sock that eventually came out the other end in a nice coil. It took quite a bit of washing to put that sock back to use, I can tell you."

"Are you serious?" asked Rose.

Angela was laughing again. "No – not about washing the sock anyway. The rest is true though. Then there's also that border collie whose kennel you just cleaned out. She came to us just yesterday – poisoned. Apparently she'd jumped into someone's backyard just a few blocks from here and ate a whole bottle of phenol red – you know the stuff they use to test for pH in swimming pools?"

"Oh no! Will she be alright?" asked Valerie.

"Well luckily phenol red isn't all that toxic. It just acts as a pretty strong laxative. It stains the faeces red too."

"I thought that was blood," remarked Rose.

"No – thankfully," said Angela. "Okay, so it seems to me you want a large dog, but one that doesn't need too much walking or stimulation – am I right?"

"Yeah – I'm in school and Mum's at work. But when I'm home, I want to have... a companion – someone to hang around with me all the time, like when I'm studying for exams. I get... lonely."

"Well come this way – I think we might just have a match," said Angela, pointing to the main complex.

Inside they found a large golden retriever, lying down on its stretcher bed. Clearly everything had just been cleaned: Rose could smell the same disinfectant she had just used.

"Evan's just been here cleaning out Sally's kennel – haven't you Evan?"

"Yes, that I have," said Evan, opening up the caged door. "Come here sweetie," he called, tapping his thighs and Sally, who had been lazily thumping her tail against the bed, got up slowly, stretched lazily, and ambled towards Evan where she stopped and, panting heavily, let Evan scratch her behind the ears.

Rose opened the cage door and eased herself in. As soon as she did so, Sally abruptly broke free to approach her, promptly sitting down on her haunches directly in front of Rose staring up at her with watery eyes. Rose reached under her chin (as Evan had instructed her) and felt the soft fur, then stroked the dog's silken ears. Sally's tongue flickered out and licked Rose's hand.

After a minute, the large dog abruptly flopped onto its back. "She wants you to rub her tummy," said Evan. "I think she likes you."

So Rose spent the next few minutes rubbing Sally's belly with the dog closing her eyes, seemingly dozing off. Except whenever Rose stopped the rubbing, Sally would open one eye and paw her gently to continue. Rose laughed, as did the others.

"What's Sally's story?" asked Valerie.

"She's seven years old and de-sexed — a pure-bred golden retriever. Like many in her breed, she suffers from a congenital hip dysplasia, although it is mild in her case and so far the vet hasn't recommended surgery. We're trying to manage it by controlling her weight. As you can see, retrievers get quite big — and Sally loves her food. The other thing she needs is a daily dose of non-steroidal anti-inflammatories. In the future, she might need surgery, which could cost a few thousand dollars —

but we can't say for sure."

"Why is she at the shelter?" asked Valerie.

"Her family was in a car accident. Basically there was no one to look after her. The neighbours brought her here. Because of her health problems, no one wants her, so she's on borrowed time."

"Well I want her," said Rose immediately. She was still rubbing Sally's belly.

"Honey, are you sure? She's not exactly the dog you described to me yesterday…" said Valerie gently.

"Yes Mum, I'm sure," replied Rose, without looking back. "She's perfect."

"Rose sweetheart – Sally's not exactly a 'guard dog', now is she?" noted Valerie. When Angela raised an eyebrow, Valerie explained quietly: "Rosie feels a bit afraid when she's alone at night." Angela nodded and Valerie turned back to her daughter. "Rosie – Sally might need a lot more care than we can give her…"

"I'll give her plenty," said Rose.

"Let me guess: you'll pay for everything," laughed her mother. Then she said to Angela: "Okay then: it looks like Sally has found a new home."

"So – I guess I'll see you next Friday," said Evan, leaning against his car.

They were in the driveway of Rose's and Valerie's house. Valerie had already gone inside. Rose was standing opposite Evan with Sally glued to her side, letting Rose scratch her ears. "Yeah. Hey, thanks Evan – for everything. I had a great time," she said.

"I'm glad it worked out," said Evan with a smile. "I wasn't sure what to expect this morning."

"Oh…" said Rose remembering. "I'm sorry about that. I don't know what you heard…"

"Not much. You were obviously having a row with your mum. It happens."

"Yeah well…"

"Is that why she came along?"

"What do you mean?" asked Rose.

"To the shelter. I heard your mum say something about me being a 'strange young man'."

Rose felt her cheeks going hot. "She didn't mean that. She's just been worried about me. We've… had a hard time lately."

"I had a feeling," said Evan, almost to himself.

"What do you mean by that?" Rose asked, frowning.

"Hm? Oh, nothing."

"Go on – say it!"

"Oh – the sudden changes in your mood. The Goth thing on Wednesday – seeing you smoking. It just seemed out of character. I thought… I don't know what I thought. I should keep my mouth shut and mind my own business," Evan said backing away.

"No – it's okay," said Rose abruptly. "You're right.

Could you tell that to my mum?"

Evan frowned. "What do you mean?"

"Tell her what you just told me. Exactly that."

Evan shook his head slowly. "I'm sorry Rose: whatever it is you want me to say, I can't get involved – it's between you and your mother. Especially when I've only just met Valerie. I want her to like me…"

"Well she does," Rose blurted out. "I mean, you talked so much on the way back. I know Mum. She'll listen to you."

Evan grimaced. "You'll work things out with your mother. I know you will. You don't need me blundering in. I'll just stuff things up. Besides: your mum's happy right now – look how she went inside humming to herself. And you've both got Sally: she'll break any tension in the house. How can she not?" Evan knelt down and gave Sally a scratch under the chin. "See ya soon old girl. You look after Rose and Valerie eh?" Then he got up, suddenly gave Rose a peck on the cheek, smiled, got in his car and drove off.

When Rose walked to the front door she was surprised that she didn't even have to call Sally: her new friend stuck by her, stride for stride.

But once inside, Sally felt free to roam. In fact, she seemed intent on sniffing every inch of the house – starting at the front door and moving along the skirting board. She inhaled the old floral carpet, breathed the mouldy odour of the wallpaper in the corridor, savoured the polished scent of the ancient jarrah doorframe to the lounge and lingered over the couch and the seats. To her, every banal object seemed to hold endless fascination. She paid particular interest to Tony's old recliner.

Rose was watching Sally as she conducted her investigation, her tail wagging so hard it knocked over the lamp on the side stand (luckily, it got caught between the chair and the heavy drapes so that it didn't fall to the ground).

Eventually Rose became aware that her mother was standing at the entrance to the dining room, leaning against the door frame, her head cocked to one side, a smile dimpling her cheeks. Their gazes met and Rose couldn't help smiling too.

"Are you happy Rose," asked Valerie.

"Yes," she replied, beaming. As if summoned, Sally rushed up to Rose, quickly licked her hand, then resumed her exploration. "Will she always be like this?" she asked, watching Sally run into the corridor.

"No sweetheart. She'll calm down soon enough – you'll see. Have you left your bedroom door open?"

"Yes I have."

"Good. Let her sniff everywhere. She needs to go into every nook and cranny. After that, she'll probably be so exhausted she'll just want to sleep."

Rose laughed, peering into the corridor to see what Sally was up to.

Valerie said: "You realise that golden retrievers shed a lot of hair?"

"Mm-hm," said Rose.

"That means a lot more vacuuming." mused Valerie.

"I don't mind," her daughter replied, still staring at Sally. "I'll do it."

Valerie scoffed, saying: "I'm going to hold you to that," but Rose didn't reply: she was too busy staring at her pet, a smile etched into her face. After a while Valerie said: "You know, I saw you outside."

"When?" asked Rose absently, her gaze still fixed on her dog. She was half in the lounge and half in the hallway.

"Around the time Evan was leaving. I was here opening up the drapes."

"Uh-huh." Rose was still grinning as Sally disappeared into Valerie's bedroom.

"I saw Evan kiss you."

Rose looked back suddenly. "Oh Mum!"

"Well I didn't mean to spy… I was just there when it happened."

"Oh please! You were spying!"

Valerie, who was still leaning on the dining room door frame, started laughing. Despite herself, Rose couldn't help but start to do the same – even as she threw a cushion from the couch which completely missed her mother, hitting an old painting of a sailing ship and knocking it askew.

"I'm sorry – I shouldn't tease," apologised Valerie, trying her best to stifle her laughter by covering her mouth.

"No – you shouldn't," scolded Rose. "Evan was just saying goodbye, that's all."

"Oh really? Is that how he says goodbye at work?" asked Valerie falling into another bout of laughter.

Rose pursed her lips and was about to say something when Sally abruptly started to bark – a deep, full-throated roar that punctuated an otherwise continuous, low growl. Rose and Valerie both froze. But when they rushed into the corridor the barking and growling suddenly stopped and Sally was nowhere to be seen. They raced to the bedrooms, each of them checking her own, but the dog was in neither. Then the growling started up again – a rumble that could be felt vibrating through the floorboards. It was coming from the entrance hallway.

They both arrived, breathless, to find Sally staring up at the old metal staircase, her hackles raised, teeth bared and muscles tense.

"What is it girl?" asked Rose as she gingerly approached the snarling dog. She reached out to touch her but reconsidered. Sally's glare was fixed, unflinchingly, on the trapdoor at the stop of the staircase. "Mum... someone is up there!" said Rose at last.

"Don't be silly! Sally's just excited. It's probably a just a mouse."

Sally barked again, the sound booming as it resonated off the walls and up into the stairwell.

"Mum, she's trying to tell us something!" yelled Rose above the noise.

"She's just getting used to the place," yelled back Valerie, however her words were largely drowned out by the barking.

Rose stepped cautiously onto the first step of the staircase, but Sally pushed herself in front, stopping Rose from getting any higher.

Abruptly Sally stopped both her barking and growling: now she had reverted to sniffing and panting. Eventually the dog turned around, looking for a way to climb down – except Rose was in the way.

"See – just a false alarm," said Valerie as Sally slipped past Rose and ambled back into the corridor.

It was much later that same night and Rose was in her bedroom listening to the familiar rasp of her mother's snore through the walls. Once again, she was holding an anti-depressant tablet in the palm of her hand, having just pushed it out of the blister pack. She was wondering whether she should take it or not. The part of her that felt she should do it was winning.

Just minutes before, Rose had finished counting her money: it was all there, minus the six hundred dollars she'd paid for Sally. Her funds had more than halved in recent weeks. Valerie was right: her money wasn't going to stretch very far at all – not with doctor's fees and medication costs.

Rose glanced up at Sally who was lying next to her and the golden retriever's eyebrows twitched one way then the other as she studied her mistress' face. Rose felt secure for the first time in a very long time. She reached out and stroked the dog's silken ears. Sally closed her eyes and sighed in a low murmur.

Rose started thinking about her memory – how she could no longer trust it at all. Had any of the strange events happened? Could she have confused shifts? Was she hearing and seeing things that weren't there? Even those entries in her journal were obviously done by her own hand: mental illness was the only reasonable explanation in the circumstances. But then there was the vexing question of the missing $106.00 from Friday night. Where could that have gone? Where might she have put it while being the 'other Rose'? She thought she'd looked everywhere.

Suddenly Rose had an idea: whenever she had stolen

things in the past (they'd only caught her three times – there had been many other occasions), the contraband had always gone into her undies drawer. Had she just stolen from herself?

Sally picked up her head with interest as Rose headed to her chest of drawers. She rifled through it looking for money but found nothing.

Then a metallic glint at the back of the top drawer caught her eye. Rose pulled it out. It was a rose-gold watch with a pearl inlay and art-deco numerals – just the kind of style Rose loved. But where had it come from?

Much to Sally's alarm, Rose scrambled under the bed to grab her journal, flicking to the last page. This time, she found a sketch of the watch. And a sentence – again, in her own handwriting – that said:

'I hope you enjoyed the date I set up with Evan.
And I got you a present.'

Rose closed the journal and held it with trembling hands. What had she – or the other Rose – been up to?

Whatever this was, it had to stop – right now. And Rose knew what she had to do.

Innocent

The first thing Rose did was push the anti-depressant tablet back into its blister pack and shove the box under her bed again.

Then Rose took her journal to her desk and wrote a new entry underneath the one from the other Rose. It read:

> 'Thanks, but I don't want your present. Please take it back. And please stop interfering in my life – you're not helping, you're just making things worse. Goodbye.'

Below that Rose drew a caricature of herself waving.

When she was finished, she carefully tore out the entire last page, removing both her own message and that from the other Rose. Finally, she grabbed the gold watch and wrapped it carefully in the torn journal paper, sealing the package with a single piece of sticky tape. Sally watched all of this with great interest, sitting on her haunches, her ears pricked up.

"Okay Sal – it's crunch time. Are you ready?" asked

Rose. Sally did no more than tilt her head curiously, so Rose added: "Good then. Let's do it."

The noise of Valerie's snoring was suddenly amplified as Rose poked her head out into the dark corridor. That was because Valerie's room had its door slightly ajar. Valerie never closed her door fully, telling her daughter once: "My parents used to shut me out of their room but I'm never going to do that to you."

As she tip-toed down the corridor, Rose wondered, not for the first time, whether her mother needed to see a sleep specialist about her breathing at night: it really didn't sound healthy once you got up close. However as far as tonight went, Valerie's snoring was a good thing: it meant Rose had fair warning that her mother was asleep. Obviously, Valerie would not approve of what her daughter was about to do. And besides, Rose was anxious to avoid her mother ever discovering the existence of the watch. It was clearly expensive and Valerie would know Rose hadn't bought it. Which left only one alternative...

So Rose and Sally groped their way in the darkness, the pale moonlight through the front door serving as their only guide. (Rose had her torch, but decided against using it in the corridor: she would save that for the ventilation room.)

Suddenly she heard Valerie sigh deeply and turn over

in her creaky bed. Both girl and dog froze. Rose's heart skipped an extra beat when she also heard Valerie's disembodied voice exclaim something in the darkness. It took a moment before she realised that her mother was sleep-talking. So Rose stayed there in the shadows, utterly immobile, listening to her heart pounding in her chest. It was only when the snoring resumed a few minutes later that Rose allowed herself to inch forward again. Sally patiently followed at her mistress' heel.

But as fast as Rose's heart had been racing, this barely compared to the moment she reached the bottom of the staircase. In fact, her pulse rate rose so rapidly that the thumping in her temples made her dizzy. Of course, the dizziness only got worse as she started the creaky climb to the top of the staircase.

Sally dutifully stayed by her side and, unlike the previous day, didn't seem at all perturbed by the ascent to the attic: rather, she was excited, and was sniffing the air expectantly. The only issue for the golden retriever was climbing the steep stairs: Rose worried a few times that Sally's gammy hips might make her slip on the narrow steps. Luckily Sally was quite content to take her time, shuffling each foot separately as she climbed – which also matched Rose's effort to climb as quietly as she could.

By the time they got to the trapdoor, the pulse in Rose's head had morphed into something resembling a deafening nightclub bassline. Rose gritted her teeth, held her breath and clenched her eyes shut as she pressed attic light switch, then listened intently for any reaction in the room above – however, the attic remained silent. Eventually, Rose summoned up the courage to push the trapdoor upwards.

The single light bulb hung still in the centre of the room – which made Rose feel instantly reassured: the door to the ventilation room was probably closed. And that is precisely what Rose saw once she climbed up into the room. The attic was exactly as she had last left it: the sights and smells brought a flood of memories, most of them unwelcome, and Rose did her best to push them out of her mind, focusing on Sally who was having some difficulty pulling her back legs up onto the floor from the top step but seemed determined to scrabble her way up nonetheless. Rose bent down to help but only succeeded in getting scratched on her arm by Sally's desperate clawing: in the end, the dog managed it on her own.

So they stood there for a few minutes – girl and dog – surveying the closed ventilation room door, with Rose hyperventilating from stress and Sally panting from the exertion of climbing the stairs.

After a few minutes Rose finally mustered the courage to walk up and grasp the chrome-plated handle, seeing her distorted reflection grow on its surface as she approached. She abruptly pulled the door wide open, stepping back and flinching instinctively as she did so.

She was greeted by silent blackness.

Rose flicked on her torch and shone it into the room, instantly capturing millions of floating dust particles in the beam. But aside from the foil-covered air-conditioning unit, the space was empty.

Sally was sniffing and wanted to go inside but Rose put her hand out and stopped her.

"Stay Sally," she said quietly, and the dog obeyed instantly, sitting down at Rose's side and looking up at her mistress as she awaited further instructions.

With trembling hands, Rose took the packaged watch and bent down so as to climb through the low door frame, leaving one foot out in the attic – just in case.

Once inside the room, Rose carefully placed the package on the ground just to the left of the door, seeing it sink slightly into a pile of fine dust that covered the floor.

As soon as she'd done that, Rose exited as quickly as she could (in fact, she did it a little too quickly since she managed to bang her head on the frame as she swung herself out). Then she pushed the door shut, making sure that she heard the door handle click. She wanted to repeat the opening and closing twice more for good measure, but something told her it wouldn't be a good idea. Maybe she was winning her war with her compulsions? Who would have thought?

Standing back, Rose knew she still had to do more: she needed to lock the door somehow. Sadly, the lever door handle didn't have any sort of locking mechanism. So Rose scanned the room, considering her options.

Eventually she bent down to whisper to Sally: "At the risk of waking Mum, I think we'll have to move the wardrobe over the door." She scratched under her dog's chin. "What do you think girl?" Sally gave her a lick on the face.

So Rose spent the next fifteen minutes inching the heavy wardrobe over the floorboards, squeaking the heavy wood this way and that, pausing every few seconds to listen for interruptions to Valerie's breathing until at last she was finished and the wardrobe was in place, blocking the ventilation room door.

By that time, Rose was drenched in sweat: despite the relatively cool night, the attic had trapped enough heat from the day to make it a few degrees warmer than downstairs. And Rose wasn't entirely sure she was sweating just from physical exertion anyway.

She sat down on the lumpy old foam bed and yawned. Sally lay down at her feet and did the same. Rose's pyjamas were not only soaked through, they were also covered in dirt and cobwebs. She'd need a shower. But at least the job was done: the other Rose might try to open the ventilation room door but it would hit the back of the wardrobe, opening no more than a millimetre. That would be it – the wardrobe was far too heavy to knock over, after all.

This meant that the other Rose was now effectively locked out (or was that 'in'?). And, as far as Rose was concerned, that was how it was going to stay.

"What were you doing up last night? I dimly remember hearing some kind of racket. In fact, I could have sworn it was coming from the attic." Valerie was making herself a coffee when Rose walked in, bleary-eyed, her hair looking like a bird's nest. Sally was shadowing her, of course.

"Attic?" said Rose. "That must have been the other Rose," she replied smirking as she opened the fridge.

"Not funny Rose. Did you go up there?"

"No," lied Rose. "Of course not. I did have another shower though."

"Why?"

"I just felt dirty. After the whole day – you know?"

"You and your OCD. Have you talked to Dr. Clarke about that?" asked Valerie.

"Yes Mum. And it's getting better, so stop worrying."

"I see you took your tablet – you look all dopey."

"Gee – thanks Mum."

"You're welcome dear," said her mother, walking

over and giving her a kiss on the forehead. "I'm proud of you. Anyway, how's our Sally?" she said stooping to pat the dog.

"She's great. I loved having her in my room."

"Have you let her out to go to the toilet this morning?" asked Valerie.

"Uh-huh. All done."

"Good girl. So – what do you have planned for today?"

"I dunno. I have some chemistry stuff I've got to do. An assignment. I've been re-partnered since… since the whole Jennifer Chiong thing went sour."

"Oh…" said Valerie.

"Don't worry – it's okay. I got this guy Sumant. He's good. And we get along," continued Rose, putting Weetbix into her bowl and pouring some milk.

"Now I do have to ask you: what in the world did you do to your pyjamas? I did a wash this morning and they were filthy – and damp!"

"I decided to clean up a bit – under my bed."

"When?"

"Before my shower."

"You're a nutter, you know that?"

"Mum…"

"Sorry – figure of speech."

"You're so inappropriate sometimes," said Rose, putting a spoonful of cereal in her mouth.

"I know – our generation didn't learn all your politically correct language," replied Valerie. She frowned saying the last few words because she was looking down the entrance hall. "Say Rose, were you expecting anyone?"

"On Sunday morning? No. Why?"

"A car is pulling into our driveway." As if on cue, Rose heard the engine noise, the crunch of tyres on gravel and a handbrake pull up. Sally started barking, the noise echoing in the kitchen.

A moment later footsteps were heard on the porch, then a knock on the door. Two figures stood outside, their outlines skewed by the scattered light of the glass. The dog's barking intensified.

"Sally – come here," ordered Rose. The dog dutifully obeyed. "Oh Mum – I'm not even dressed!"

"Don't worry – you finish your breakfast. Probably Jehovah's Witnesses. I'll deal with it," said Valerie.

Rose kept eating with one hand while holding onto Sally's collar with the other (just in case). As she chewed, she heard the door being opened and the low murmur of voices. Whoever it was went on talking for some time – for long enough for Rose to realise that her mother's coffee was getting cold. Eventually, the voices started moving down the corridor. Sally's tail was wagging so furiously so that her body movement was threatening to knock Rose off her stool.

Valerie entered the kitchen first, followed by two uniformed police officers – a woman and a man.

"Rose, I'll need you to get dressed and join us in the lounge sweetheart. As soon as you can…" Her mother was ashen-faced.

"What's happened?"

"The officers will explain. They… they need to ask you some questions."

Rose knew what it was about of course but tried not to think about it, pulling on her old jeans and a sweater. She'd need practical clothes if she was going to be taken down to the station. After getting dressed, she snuck into the bathroom to brush her teeth quickly. Again: there was no sense in having smelly breath, and bits of cereal caught in her teeth, while she was being questioned.

Finally she walked into the lounge where the two officers were waiting. Rose could see that her mother had made herself a fresh cup of coffee and was drinking it with shaky hands. No doubt she'd offered coffee to the officers, but they had politely refused.

"Hello Rose," said the female officer, "please have a seat." The male officer smiled but said nothing.

Rose sat on the couch opposite the constables while Sally approached them and allowed herself to be patted.

"Rose… we need to ask you some questions," said the female officer. Her name badge read 'Simpson'.

Rose stared at them but said nothing, feeling her heart-rate rising.

"Where were you yesterday at about 11:35 a.m.?" asked Constable Simpson.

Rose looked at her mother then back to the officer. "I was with my Mum. We were up in Kalamunda – at the animal shelter there."

The male officer, who was patting Sally, smiled sadly and shook his head. "We have reason to suspect that you're not telling us the truth."

"She was there – with me!" interjected Valerie.

"Please, Mrs. Azzopardi," replied the officer. His name badge read 'Davis'. "We need to hear from Rose first."

"I… I was up there. With Mum. We left early – at about a quarter to eight in the morning. We… came home after two in the afternoon," stammered Rose.

"The problem is," said Constable Simpson, "we have a photo that looks an awful lot like you. It's a still picture taken from CCTV footage. And if it is you, then you weren't at that animal shelter – you were somewhere else."

Rose blurted out: "I didn't do it!"

"Didn't do what Rose?" asked Constable Simpson quietly.

"Whatever it is I'm supposed to have done. Stolen something I suppose."

"We didn't mention anything being stolen," said Constable Davis.

"You didn't need to. I've been caught three times for shoplifting – right? Now you guys think I've shoplifted again. Well I haven't! My mum can tell you. We were in Kalamunda all morning yesterday!"

Constable Davis took out a piece of paper from his pocket, unfolded it and handed it to Rose. "Are you saying that this isn't you?"

Rose took the print and examined it with trembling hands. Valerie came to look over her shoulder. It was a photo taken at a shopping centre – she couldn't tell which one – outside a jeweller's. The photo was unremarkable – a young woman walking, wearing Gothic clothing and make-up. The problem was, she looked exactly like Rose.

And the date and time stamp at the bottom of the picture read: '11:28 05-11-2016'.

"No," said Rose, shaking her head. She looks like me. But she's someone else. I don't know her."

Constable Simpson sighed deeply, pursing her lips. "Rose… I'm afraid we're going to have to take you down to the station with us for further questioning."

"Why? I told you – it isn't me!"

"We both reviewed the CCTV footage this morning. It shows a young woman going into a jeweller's shop. She tries on a watch. And when the shop assistant is distracted, she runs off without paying for it. That still picture you've got in your hands is from footage taken just before the theft. But there are cameras everywhere in the centre. And I'm afraid all of them point to you. Our facial recognition software matched you from our database to practically every image we could find. So you see, we haven't really got a choice."

"That's impossible. She was with me the whole morning," interjected Valerie.

"With respect, Mrs. Azzopardi – you're Rose's mother. And we know you had your licence suspended recently. You couldn't have driven Rose anywhere yesterday – at least, not legally," said Constable Simpson, getting up slowly and indicating that Rose should do so as well.

"Well it's true that I didn't drive anywhere," said Valerie. "A young man named Evan drove us. He works with Rose at a restaurant here in Mount Hawthorn – Valentino's – but he's also a volunteer at the Kalamunda Wildlife Shelter – which is where we went."

"Mrs. Azzopardi, that's something Rose's lawyer can raise at the trial…" said Constable Davis.

"There won't be any trial!" said Valerie firmly. "If you even try to arrest, never mind charge, my daughter, I'll sue you both for malicious prosecution! What kind of 'investigation' is this anyway? You haven't even asked the manager of the wildlife centre to verify Rose's alibi!

Here…" said Valerie frantically rifling through her handbag until she found Angela's card which she pushed into Constable Simpson's hands. "Go and see her. She'll tell you we were there yesterday. So will a whole lot of other people who work at the shelter."

"And Evan will too," added Rose.

"Take a photo of us now and show it to them. Go on! And make sure you include the dog that you're patting," said Valerie, pointing to Constable Davis. "After all – where do you think we got her from?"

The two officers looked at each other and Constable Simpson slowly sat down again.

"Are you saying that you went up to this animal shelter to get this dog?"

"No. We went up with Evan to volunteer for the morning. Our names will be on the register as visitors. Afterwards, Rose saw Sally and wanted us to adopt her – so we did. All of the paperwork will confirm that too."

"And this took place between which hours?" asked Constable Davis.

"Rose tried to tell you: we left at around 7:45 a.m. and got back after 2:00 p.m. That means we would have been at the shelter from between 8:20 a.m. to 1:15 p.m. Yet you say this theft took place at 11:35 a.m. Rose would need to be criminal mastermind to have faked an alibi as rock-solid as that!" exclaimed Valerie. She was breathing heavily – almost hyperventilating – as she finished her sentence.

Constable Simpson raised her eyebrows slowly and looked at Constable Davis. He simply shrugged. "Very well," she said after a pause. "We'll take a photo of the three of you – and use it to make further enquiries. We'll get back to you after that. Do you have contact details for this… 'Evan'?" asked Constable Simpson turning to Rose.

She nodded as she pulled out her phone. "I'll text them to you."

"No – just write them down please. I'm a bit old-fashioned that way," said Constable Simpson with a smile, handing Rose a card and pen.

A moment later Rose, Valerie and Sally posed stiffly for a photo in the lounge room. As they were lining up, Rose noticed that the painting of the sailing ship behind them was still skew. She desperately wanted to straighten it but she stopped herself anyway. Another win against her OCD.

Constable Davis took the picture with his phone then showed it to Constable Simpson who nodded, saying: "Okay then, we'll be in touch – hopefully later today." She smiled faintly and headed for the door. Constable Davis followed, stopping briefly to pat Sally again.

Rose and her mother watched from the lounge window as the police car did a three-point turn then disappeared down the driveway. Only then did Valerie turn to her daughter and say:

"We need to talk about what you were up to last night. And this time, I want the truth."

Rose stared numbly out of the window, wondering what to say. But Valerie wasn't going anywhere: she stood with her arms crossed, her brow furrowed and her eyes focused intently on her daughter. In the end Rose simply said: "I had to get rid of the watch."

"Watch?" exclaimed her mother. "How in the world did you get the watch in the first place?"

"It's part of a bigger story that I've been trying to tell you Mum – for ages. You just won't listen!"

"Well I'm listening now. Start talking. How did you get the watch? Who is this girl?"

"So you believe me now – that there is another girl?" asked Rose.

Valerie sighed. "Yes – of course. How can I not? The police have just showed us a picture of her in some shopping mall – taken at time when you were with me up in the hills."

"So then you know that this 'other Rose' must have gone to the Chiongs' party, worked on Wednesday for me – all of it!"

"Yes sweetheart – I know. Just please – get on with it: how did you get the watch?"

Rose exhaled and shook her head. "Everyone's been

telling me I was going crazy. Well I wasn't!"

Valerie put her hands on her daughter's cheeks, looked into her eyes and said: "Look Rosie – I know. I was wrong. And I'm sorry. Really I am. But right now I need you to help me understand what is happening. We just had the police here, for crying out loud. Please – help me understand!"

"Okay…" said Rose as she collected her thoughts. "Basically I was in my bedroom last night, working up the courage to take my medication. But I put it off and decided to count my money instead."

"Yes, yes," said Valerie rotating her hand. "I know how you count your damn money. Get to the point sweetheart or you'll be the death of me."

"I am getting to the point! Anyway, I noticed the other day that $106.00 was missing. So I figured that my 'other' personality must have taken it. In other words, I thought I must have stolen from myself."

"And…?" Valerie waved her hand in a circle again.

"I decided to look for the money where I used to hide the things I stole."

"Hide the things you stole? How many other things have you stolen exactly?"

"Oh Mum – now isn't the time or the place to get into that! Look, I went to the top drawer – my undie drawer – that's where I used to hide stuff. Only I didn't find the money there. Instead I found this beautiful gold watch."

"Gold watch – the one that just got stolen?"

"Yes."

Valerie scratched her head and paced. "This doesn't make any sense at all. Go back a step – what was the story behind your missing money?"

"The $106.00? Well that was the money that the other Rose took for working my Wednesday shift."

"Oh honey… I had a bad feeling when I asked you about this. You're not making any sense at all…"

"You have to believe me Mum! Come – I'll show you," insisted Rose, grabbing her mother by the hand and leading her to her bedroom.

A few minutes later Valerie, who had finished reading her daughter's journal, looked up and asked: "Are you trying to tell me that this 'other Rose' worked for you on Wednesday, then paid herself out of your pot of money?" She was sitting next to her daughter on the bed.

"Yes Mum. That's what I'm saying," replied Rose. I used to get paid in cash – now it all goes into my bank account. The other Rose didn't know about that. Apparently she got quite cross and argued with Sofia."

Valerie nodded but seemed lost in concentration, biting her lip as she studied the pages of the journal, flipping between the drawing of Jon at the Halloween party and the drawing of the flying fifty dollar notes. Eventually she said: "Something's missing here. You've torn a page out at the end. What was on it?"

"That's the part I hadn't finished explaining. After I found the watch, I went straight to the journal to see if I'd gotten a new message from the other Rose – you know, like the one she left me when she took money from my pot. Well it turned out that she had left me a new message: she'd drawn a picture of the watch I found in my drawer – and written a note which said something like: 'I hope you enjoyed your 'date' with Evan and also, I left you a present.'"

"Obviously the present was the watch..." said Valerie.

"I think the picture made that pretty clear Mum."

"Okay – so how did the other Rose know about your 'date' with Evan then?" asked Valerie frowning and scratching her scalp.

"Because she was the one who organised it on Wednesday. I didn't know anything about the 'date' because I wasn't there. By the time I went to work on Friday, everyone was laughing at me for being a Goth and smoking. Then Evan started talking to me about my promise to visit the shelter on Saturday. Of course, I had no idea what he meant, so I just played along. Remember – both you and Patricia had been telling me that the other Rose and I were the same person: that I just didn't remember some of the things I'd said and done. So what other choice did I have? That's why I didn't even realise the visit was going to be all about doing volunteer work," said Rose.

"You just thought you were going to look for a pet..." mused Valerie.

"Well, I didn't really think about it at all, to be honest. It's just that Evan... he keeps inviting me to things. So I kind of guessed he liked me. I thought he was just looking for an excuse to ask me out to something – anything. And since I really did want a dog, it seemed..."

"Like a good opportunity to get what you wanted," finished Valerie. "Hm. You were using Evan a bit, don't you think? But we'll have to leave that for another time. Right now, I need you to tell me what you did after that."

"As soon as I finished reading the note from the other Rose, I wrote her a reply, saying I didn't want her present and that she should take it back. I wrote it directly underneath her entry on the same page in my journal. I drew a picture of me waving goodbye. Then I tore that page out – that's the one that's missing – and I wrapped up the watch in it. Then I left the package for the other Rose to pick up."

"Where?" asked Valerie.

"Where else? I put it just inside the ventilation room."

"Oh my word..." said Valerie putting her head in her

hands and slumping forward. "You mean it's still here? We have stolen property in this house?"

"We might. Or maybe the other Rose has already taken it away."

"Oh honey," said Valerie grabbing her daughter by the arms. "Don't you realise? We locked the house up when we left. How could this other Rose even get into the attic? That makes no sense at all!"

"None of this makes sense Mum. I mean, how did the other Rose get to my journal, my pot of money or my top drawer? After all, we locked the house when we went to Kalamunda, didn't we? It's just as difficult to get to my bedroom as it is to get to the attic."

"True. But what made you leave the watch up there? What's so special about the attic?"

"I don't know..." answered Rose. "First of all, I knew you wouldn't find it – and that was good, because if you had, you'd have chucked a fit," answered Rose (Valerie grimaced at this). "But second of all, that's where the other Rose keeps going – where I hear her at night: I hear her coughing and bumping into things. Sometimes I hear the ventilation room door being opened and other times I hear it being closed. Basically, I think that's how she gets into the house."

"She gets in the house through the ventilation room?" asked Valerie, her eyes going wide.

"Yes. Dad used to say: 'Once you eliminate the

impossible, whatever remains, no matter how improbable, must be the truth.'"

"Rose, I think you'll find that was a quote from Sherlock Holmes. Your Dad just borrowed it. But more importantly, using the ventilation room as some sort of 'entry'... sounds pretty impossible."

"Mum, everything about this is impossible. But the only way any of it makes sense is if you see that ventilation room as... a kind of door. Maybe it has a secret passage – I don't know."

"Have you looked inside?" asked Valerie.

"Yes. No. Not really. I mean, I've had a quick look. Just not a proper one. I've been too afraid," admitted Rose.

Valerie pondered the issue for a few minutes, biting her lip again. "Okay – let's assume you're right about this whole 'secret passage' thing. That means she could be up in the attic right now – listening to us. She might have walked down the staircase while we've been in here talking."

"Nuh-uh, Mum!" announced Rose proudly. Last night I made sure she couldn't."

"How?"

"I pushed the wardrobe in front of the door," said Rose.

"So that's what that noise was! I knew you were up to something!" exclaimed Valerie. Abruptly she got up and extended her hand to her daughter.

"Where are we going?" asked Rose.

"To the attic. You're going to show me where you put the watch – and we'll see if we can find this 'secret passage'. Don't worry – there are three of us now, remember: you, me and Sally."

The golden retriever tilted her head at the mention of her name.

Worlds

It was funny really: standing there with her mother and Sally on either side, the attic suddenly seemed so boring to Rose – so ordinary – that the fuss of the previous few weeks seemed totally misplaced. Once again Rose started doubting herself. And, the more she thought about it, the more she saw that there were good reasons for that doubt. Because there, up against the far wall, blocking the ventilation room door, stood the large old marri wardrobe. It symbolised one of two things: either a fantastical mystery or, more simply, Rose's growing mental illness. Given the choices, things didn't look good. In fact, Rose fully expected that she and her mother would pull aside the wardrobe only to find the watch still inside the ventilation room, lying in the dust just where Rose had left it.

Valerie surveyed the scene silently, a tightness visible in her jawline. Rose remembered just how much her mother hated being up there.

"You moved that all by yourself eh?" said Valerie at last.

"Um… yeah. Well, it's not as if Sally could help."

Valerie shook her head and smiled. "I have no idea how in the world you managed to do that – especially without me realising what you were up to. As I said before, I dimly remember hearing something last night – but I would never have guessed it was this."

"Well, I just pivoted the wardrobe this way and that. It took a while. A long while, actually," said Rose, pointing to the fresh scratch marks on the wooden floorboards which showed how the wardrobe had been dragged, pushed and inched into place. Valerie walked up to the marks and squatted down.

"You've always been very resourceful and determined – I'll give you that, Rose Azzopardi. I suppose this is how you got your pyjamas so sweaty and dirty."

"Mm-hm. It was pretty dusty behind there. I don't know if anyone has moved the wardrobe in ages."

"They probably haven't for as many as seventy years," suggested Valerie, standing up and running her hands along the ancient wood. "Oh well – time to drag it back. You ready?"

Ten minutes later, with both of them sweating and panting, the wardrobe was back where it used to be, a fresh set of bright scuff-lines and whirlpools carved into the dark wooden floor and a few splinters taken out of some of the more rotten boards.

"Okay," said Valerie stretching her sore back. "The moment of truth. Do you have your torch?"

"Yes Mum," said Rose, handing it to her.

Valerie looked at her daughter, raised her eyebrows, then pulled the door open, shining the torch beam inside. Rose held her breath until she heard her mother say: "It's empty – there's no one in there." Valerie flashed the torch around a bit more before she asked: "Where did you say you put the watch?"

"Just inside the door – on your left as you go in."

Valerie ducked her head under the low frame and stepped inside. Rose watched as her mother directed the beam to the floor where she squatted down, examining something. "I can see where you left the watch Rose. There's still a rectangular imprint in the dust. But the watch is gone. And I can see the finger marks of whoever picked it up too." Valerie shone the beam around the rest of the floor. "Did you walk around in here?"

"No. I only ever set one foot inside – and that was to put the watch down," replied Rose. "Then I got out as quickly as I could. I've always been too scared to go in. I know it's silly, but…"

"Well someone has been walking around in here – a lot," interjected Valerie. "I can see my own two footprints easily enough. The rest are… someone else's," said Valerie, still squatting, shining the torch beam onto one of the prints as she examined it.

"Could they be the other Rose's footprints?" asked her daughter.

Valerie shrugged. "Well they're definitely not yours. Although your feet seem to be about the same size, these prints weren't made by any of your shoes."

"How can you tell Mum?"

Valerie wiped her nose. "As far as I can remember, you don't own a set of Doc Martens. And that's what these prints are from. I'd know a set of Doc Martens boot prints anywhere."

"How?"

Valerie laughed and looked at her daughter, silhouetted in the doorway. "Honey, when I was younger I practically lived in Doc Martens. They are all I ever wore on my feet for most of a decade."

"When was this?"

"Back in the eighties sweetheart – when I lived at home with your nan and pop: from about your age right through to the end of university. That was my 'scene' – wearing Doc Martens, Gothic clothes and makeup, listening to The Cure…"

"The who?"

"No, not The Who – they were a different rock group. The Cure was this kind of post-punk, Gothic band that I was mad about. I used to have posters of Robert Smith – he was the lead singer – covering an entire wall in my bedroom," she said, smiling as she remembered. "I played their records so often I think I drove my parents mad." When Rose looked at her mother blankly, Valerie started singing a few bars of 'The Love Cats' in a high-pitched voice.

"Hey I know that song! Geez, it's old."

Valerie laughed. Then she turned around and began a methodical examination of every square inch of the room: stamping on the floorboards, rapping her knuckles along the air-conditioning unit, squeezing the foil vent, tapping the roof beams and examining the tiles. After a few minutes she headed to the door. Rose stood aside to let her mother duck her head under the frame. "Nothing in there I'm afraid," Valerie reported as she emerged. "No gold watch. No 'secret passageway'. Nothing."

"But you still believe me – right?" pleaded Rose.

Valerie nodded, her eyes unfocused. Eventually she said: "If we're going to lock this door, we'd better do it properly. Rose, I want you to go down to the shed and find the slide bolt that your father was going to put on the side gate. It should still be in its Bunnings packet with its screws. Bring that up with the cordless drill and a five millimetre drill bit. While you're at it, bring a spare padlock. We have stacks in the shed. You know where to find all that stuff, don't you?"

"Yes," said Rose, who had often helped her father

with his handyman work. She made her way to the trapdoor but paused there, looking back.

"Go on," said Valerie. "I'll stay here and guard the door with Sally. You just hurry – okay? The sooner we can get this done, the better."

"I don't really know what's happening Mum. I was starting to think we'd find the watch – just sitting there where I left it. Now that we haven't – and there's no secret passageway – I don't know what to think…"

"I don't know what's happening either Rosie. Maybe it will all become clear to us soon – or maybe we'll never know. All we can do is take one step at a time. So let's lock this place up. After that, we'll go downstairs, have a cup of tea and try to figure it out together."

They were sitting in the lounge and Rose saw the steam rising from her mother's mug as it caught the first rays of the afternoon light starting to flood into the lounge. It would soon be time to draw the curtains to block out the sharp western sun and heat.

Valerie was staring out into the front yard – at the dead jarrah tree – when she said: "I never told you the full story of what happened between your father and me… Hopefully it'll make some sort of sense. If it doesn't… well, you'll know you're not the only one in the family who's been worried about her sanity."

Rose leaned forward to pat Sally who was panting

softly. "Is this about the argument you had with Dad?"

"Yes. And some things before that," said Valerie as she traced the outline of the hand-painted heart on the outside of her mug. "You know, we used to be a happy little family once. You probably remember the last few months more than anything but it's important to remember that we had years of being happy before that. Okay, we weren't 'blissful' or anything. Who is? We were just 'normal'. We argued a bit. Your father and I both worked a bit too hard. We probably spent too little time with you. But we tried. We really did – all of us. Your father... he ran his air-conditioning business. And he was doing really well. He'd fit up supermarkets and office buildings..." Valerie rocked back as she remembered. "He was always crawling up in tight roof spaces. So when we saw this house – 'a renovator's dream' they called it – he said we had to buy it: he desperately wanted the attic."

"I remember," said Rose. "It was going to be his 'man cave'."

"Ha! Yes. That's right. Except he never did get around to fixing it up."

"Everything was always half-finished," remembered Rose.

Valerie laughed. "Yes – that was your dad: part of his charm, you might say. Because as annoying as he could be, we were happy with him like that. You remember how he'd come home from work earlier than I did, so I'd arrive to find you two in the kitchen cooking something together? You were always experimenting. And your father was nothing if not romantic: he'd greet me with a kiss every day. Of course, he'd have a glass of wine waiting – which in retrospect probably wasn't a good idea."

"So where did it all go wrong Mum?" asked Rose.

Valerie sipped her tea, and stared out at the jarrah tree again. "It started almost exactly three years ago. I remember it so clearly: the day everything changed. I came home from work, but your father wasn't in the kitchen. I couldn't find him anywhere. I heard his phone ringing though and found it on the dining room table. I answered it. His business partner said your father hadn't turned up to work all day and hadn't answered his phone either. It was already six thirty in the evening. They were supposed to be working at this shopping mall. It was a disaster. I checked – and there were more than twenty missed calls."

Rose frowned. "So where was he?"

"I found him in the attic. I knew he'd gone up there early in the morning for some pet project. I thought he was still going to work after that. But it turned out he never did: he spent the rest of the day in the attic – sealing the wall to the air-conditioning unit," replied Valerie.

"I never did get why he did that," mused Rose.

"Me neither. He mentioned something about 'renovating' his 'man cave' but all he did was make a mess — though he tried to paint that wall, it still looked like a rush job. And it was so pointless too: even I could tell that he was blocking access to his own new air-conditioner. But at the time I thought he knew what he was doing."

Rose's eye's widened as she blurted out: "Mum! He was doing what we just did! He was closing the door!"

Valerie took another sip of her tea and nodded. "Yes sweetheart. That's right. Except he didn't just put a padlock on the door — he sealed the wall completely."

"But why?"

"To make it more permanent I suppose," answered Valerie.

Rose said: "That must mean that whatever is in there…"

"Isn't something we want to be involved with," continued her mother. "We have to remember that it drove your father to a breakdown. Now it's starting to do the same to you. Whatever is happening in that room is obviously something we need to avoid — at all costs."

At that moment, they both saw and heard the police car pulling into the driveway again.

"I saw you."

Rose was at her locker at school and the voice had come over her shoulder. She turned around to see who it was.

"Oh… Hi Jon. Saw me where?"

"At the Karrinyup Shopping Centre on Saturday."

"I wasn't in Karrinyup on Saturday…"

"Yeah well, I saw you with my own eyes."

"What did you see?"

"Everything," said Jon.

Rose shut her locker and held her books close to her chest. "Good for you," was all she could manage.

"You don't seem worried," said Jon frowning.

"Why should I be?"

"Because I saw you steal that watch. I was passing and noticed you standing there at the jeweller's. When the lady turned her back, you ran off into the crowd. Some of the staff tried to chase after you but you disappeared pretty quickly."

"Well lucky for me then, eh?" said Rose.

Jon grimaced and shook his head. "The more I find out about you, the worse it gets."

"Oh? Go on – what else have you found out?"

"Just what Nathan said about you stealing from the pharmacy."

"Hm. Did Nathan tell you how his sister watched me apologising to the chemist staff last Thursday? I suppose things like that don't make the gossip rounds – they aren't 'juicy' enough."

Jon snorted. "Well it doesn't matter does it? You can apologise all you like. It means nothing if you're just going to keep stealing stuff."

"Well I haven't," said Rose. "I don't care what you think you saw. So if you'll excuse me, I've got a class to get to."

"I could report you to the police, you know," Jon said to her retreating back. "Tell me why I shouldn't." Several other students had stopped and were listening. A little circle had formed around them.

Rose had already walked a few steps away and she stopped, combed a strand of hair from her face with her free hand and said: "I think you *should* report me. In fact, I insist. I'll even let you use my phone." She dug it out of her pocket, walked up to Jon and held it out to him. "Maybe when the police tell you to bugger off, you'll stop judging me for something you know nothing about," she said. And then she gestured to the assembled crowd adding, "And everyone else might realise that there's a good reason why I'm not in jail but still here at school – and everything is exactly the same as it ever was."

Jon's frown deepened as he held up his hands to refuse the phone, then turned and walked away.

Rose watched him leaving with a quiet sense of satisfaction. The police had, after all, confirmed her alibi: it was rock-solid. Both constables had looked perplexed when they turned up the previous afternoon to say that Rose was officially off the hook.

"I have to confess that I still find it hard to believe this isn't you," said Constable Simpson unfolding the photo printout. But we've spoken to six different people at the shelter as well as your friend Evan. They all support your story."

"So I guess we're now looking for a young woman who looks just like you," said Constable Davis, patting Sally who had gone up to him for a nuzzle.

"Good luck with your search," said Rose.

Valerie wasn't so gracious however. "Next time, do your work properly. If you come near my daughter again with something like this I promise I will sue the pants off you." She tapped her thigh and said: "Come here Sally," and the dog walked over to Valerie's side.

No one said any goodbyes as the police walked down the porch to their car and Rose vowed silently that, as far as she could help it, this would be the last time she would ever have to speak with a police officer again.

Walking up the driveway at the end of the day, Rose could smell the thick, hot odour of eucalyptus hanging in the still air – a sure sign that summer had already arrived.

When she opened the front door she was greeted by twin blasts: the frigid air-conditioning and her golden retriever, who bounded up excitedly as if her mistress been away for an entire year and not just a single school day.

"Hello Sal!" said Rose, letting her bag fall off her shoulder and kneeling to let the dog nuzzle into her body and lick her face while Rose scratched Sally behind her ears and under her chin.

After a while Rose said: "Come on Sal – let's go to our room eh?" and she stood up and started walking. She was already halfway down the corridor when she noticed Sally hadn't moved. "What's up Sal? Come here girl," she said, tapping her thigh. But Sally stood her ground. "Come on Sally. What's up?"

The dog whined.

"Do you want to go to the toilet? Ah – good girl," said Rose, walking around the metal staircase and heading towards the back door. Initially Sally followed her enthusiastically but once again stopped – this time at the foot of the stairs.

"What is it now?"

Sally whined again.

It took Rose a moment to realise what the dog wanted. She walked up to Sally and followed her gaze to the attic trapdoor. Almost immediately, Sally started shuffling her way up the steps. Rose wanted to call her down but reconsidered. After all, the ventilation room door was now locked. What harm would it do? So she let Sally lead her up, wondering what the dog was after.

A moment later, Rose and Sally were once again standing up in the airless, stifling heat of the attic. Rose was thankful she didn't have to sleep up there any more – this particular night would have been hard to get through, especially now that Rose had once again grown accustomed to the comfort of her own bedroom with all the benefits it had to offer (including ducted air-conditioning). Sally ambled her way to the ventilation room, her tail wagging energetically, and she sat down in front of its door. When her mistress didn't follow, Sally whined again. Eventually the dog jumped up onto the door, resting her forepaws against the handle and slide bolt.

"Sally – stop that!" scolded Rose, and the dog dutifully lowered herself, letting her front claws scrape down the thin layer of peach-coloured paint that Tony had applied almost three years before. Then she turned and continued to stare at Rose, her tongue hanging out to one side as she panted.

"Who's in there Sally?" Rose asked pointlessly. The dog briefly licked her lips and swallowed, then continued panting. After a moment she whined again. Finally, Rose approached the ventilation room, listening carefully for any sound of movement. When she heard none, she decided to place her cupped ear on the door. Rose was greeted with the sort of sound you get when you put a shell to your ear: a dull, distant roar that reminded her of the wind over a stormy sea. Glancing sideways she could see out of the attic window that she was, in fact, hearing the sound of the sea: the summer wind they called the 'Fremantle Doctor' had just come in from across the ocean and was now man-handling the tall eucalypts across the road, causing their sparsely-leaved branches to flail wildly. But otherwise she could hear nothing.

Rose must have spent a good couple of minutes listening like that, her face plastered sideways to the door. She looked down and could see Sally's watery eyes pleading with her – to open the door.

After retrieving the key and her torch from the wardrobe where she had left them the day before, Rose paused in front of the padlock, wondering what it was behind the door that interested Sally so much. If it were something dangerous, Sally would be barking right now. Instead, Sally's tail hadn't stopped wagging from the moment they had gotten into the attic. In the end, Rose decided she'd have to peek in and see. So, a minute or two later, Rose found herself swallowing nervously as she slid the blot across, opening the door.

Almost immediately, Rose noticed the breeze that was coming through the gaps in the rafters: a minor wind-tunnel was created when both the trapdoor and ventilation room door were open. Rose could only imagine how breezy it might be if they could open the attic window as well.

She shone her torch into the darkness and, as before, it was empty. In fact, Rose was about to close the door when Sally slipped past her and went inside.

"Sally! You bad girl – what are you up to?" Rose flashed her torch to see the golden retriever sniffing furiously at something. All around the dog, Rose could see fresh Doc Martens boot prints. "Sally, come here!" she ordered, but Sally didn't appear to hear the command: she was too busy sniffing. In the end, Rose reluctantly climbed in after her.

Standing up in the enclosed space, Rose worried that she might bang her head – the rafters were so much lower. In the end she felt her feet squelching in the mix of fine sawdust and dirt as she approached Sally. The dog moved aside as she got closer, her torch beam wavering over what was clearly a piece of paper, folded and taped. She picked it up, her fingers sinking briefly into the fine, talcum-like powder, and then removed the single piece of tape to unfold the page. It was the same one she'd used previously. The watch was missing but there was a new entry. Rose tried to keep her torch steady as she read it. It said:

'Fine. I'll keep the watch — I like it anyway. But why'd you lock the door? If you wanted me to butt out, all you had to do was ask.

Anyway, I hope this reaches you. If you don't reply, I'll know you want me to stay away for good.

In that case, have a nice life.'

At that moment Rose felt a gust of wind blowing into the room and looked up in time to see the door of the ventilation room slamming shut. Feeling her heart rate rising, Rose rushed forward and pulled down on the handle so that door swung open.

Except the attic was now in almost complete darkness — as if someone had pulled heavy curtains across the window. Of course, there were no such curtains in the attic. And, stepping through the low doorway, Rose could instantly see through the window that the afternoon sun had been replaced by a half-moon: one that bathed the attic in ghostly shades of blue. Even the houses across the road had their lights out. What had been day had become night — all in the time it took to close and open one door.

Rose didn't know what to do except move forward. She certainly wasn't going to go back into the ventilation room. She glanced down and was relieved to see Sally at her side, her eyes glowing briefly as they reflected the torch beam.

Her surroundings didn't make sense at all. How could it be night time? Had she passed out? Rose shone her torch around the attic trying to find answers – any answers. But all she found were more questions. For starters, she noticed that the bed had been stripped of all its sheets and covers, making it look like it used to in the old days – just old foam on a packing-wood base. Rose also saw that the rotten wooden boards she had thrown out were still leaning against the far wall. And the disintegrating box with the split bag of plaster was still in the middle of the room even though Rose had removed it almost three months previously. It was as if Rose had gone back in time – to before her own 'mini-renovation', before her last 'attic imprisonment'.

Except not quite.

Other details didn't fit the past or present: cardboard boxes she didn't recognise were stacked next to the sink on the other side of the toilet while a ladder was stored on its side under the window. Most importantly, the wardrobe was missing. Her torch beam explored the gap where it had once been, reflecting the cobwebs and dust she'd gotten all over her pyjamas not that long ago. She looked down to the floor and could see that the wardrobe had, at some point, been dragged to the trapdoor.

She shone the beam back up and followed the wall

across to the ventilation room door. At least that was in the same space. The problem was, it had its original brass handle – not the new chrome one the workers had installed when they had refitted the door at the start of the year. She walked up and examined it closely, feeling the curved art-deco lines, studying its familiar dull tarnish.

It was only then that she noticed that the door, and indeed the entire wall, still bore its original 'lime' colour – not the 'peach' Tony had chosen for his 'man cave makeover'. In other words, the wall was the same as it had been before Tony sealed it.

Rose heard Sally's soft panting and reached down to feel her soft silky ears and the dog licked her mistress' hands. At least Rose had one constant with her – one link to familiarity and, possibly, reality. Taking a deep breath, Rose decided to press on with her investigation, making her way gingerly to the trapdoor. What else could she do?

The steps were still in place: that much was the same. Rose and Sally slowly descended them in the dark, letting the moonlight from the front door window be their guide. Rose had decided to turn her torch off so as not to wake anyone – whoever that 'anyone' might be. It was a safe bet that Valerie was one of them – her snoring could be heard down the length and breadth of the corridor.

As they got to the bottom Rose searched for the 1970s clock. She breathed a sigh of relief when she saw it was still there, getting up very close in order to see what time it was: 3:34 a.m. As her hand touched the wall she instantly felt that the old wallpaper was gone: it had been replaced by some dark shade of paint, the colour of which Rose found impossible to make out in the pale grey moonlight. And there was more: the family photographs Valerie had collected and thrown into the bin were all still there, hanging in their original places. Rose decided to risk switching on her torch in order to examine them, but did so in her closed fist so it glowed red while a narrow shard of light escaped between her fingers.

The portraits were just as she remembered: there was the one of Mum and Dad on a beach in Broome before she was born. Next to it was the picture of Rose as a chubby baby, held by a primly dressed and seated Valerie, while Tony, with neatly combed hair and a chequered shirt, stood next to her – the family posing against a ghastly, mottled-blue 'studio' background.

Memories came flooding back as she followed the line of the other photos: Rose's ballet concert when she was five, and Tony and Valerie with Nan and Pop – all seated on the back verandah with Christmas hats, toasting... The photos were just the same as they had been three years before.

Except for the last picture: this one was new.

Rose let more of the light escape from her fingers so she could study it closely. She realised her heart was pounding and her breathing had become ragged, matching Sally's panting. The picture showed Rose in 'Gothic mode', one arm around her father on the left and the other around her mother on the right. They were standing in front of a car – a Hyundai Excel – which was parked in their driveway. No one was smiling. Rose felt the frame with her fingertips: unlike the other photos it had no dust on the top edge of its frame.

Abruptly, Rose heard a sigh – a deep one – coming from somewhere nearby. Then a creaking noise – someone moving on an old spring mattress – made Rose jump back and Sally began to growl.

"Shh!" whispered Rose harshly, but Sally continued to make a low rumble in her throat, her eyes fixed on the lounge. "Stay girl," commanded Rose as she tip-toed to the door which, for a change, had been shut. Rose opened it as slowly and quietly as she could and peeked inside.

The problem was that she couldn't see much in the shadows: the moonbeams didn't reach far enough into the room. All she could tell was that someone appeared to be on the couch against the back wall, breathing deeply and slowly in the way people do when they are fast asleep.

Suddenly, the headlights of a passing car coming down the road swept across the room in an arc, lighting it up, and Rose saw that their old couch had been replaced by some kind of fold-out bed. A man was lying on it with his back turned to her. A moment later the car was gone and the room fell back into darkness. Rose closed the door, holding her breath and trying to avoid any 'click' as she eased the handle back down.

With her heart racing, Rose held Sally by the collar as they made their way down the corridor towards the bedrooms. She passed her own room but the door was closed. Valerie's was, however, open (as usual) and Rose put her head around to peer in, seeing nothing but a dark shape on the bed and hearing her mother's snoring which, at this distance, sounded very much like the slow sawing of a log.

Rose eased her way out and was already walking back down the corridor again, her hand still firmly on Sally's collar, when a car entered the driveway. She froze as she heard the car drive up, its engine turn off, the handbrake get pulled and a car door open and slam shut. This was followed by crunching on the gravel path, heavy footsteps on the porch and the jingle of keys. Sally began to growl again – the same low rumble as before. The front door was flung open, keys were dropped onto the hallway stand and a dark figure stomped around the corner – almost walking into girl and dog. Both Rose and the stranger gasped – identically. The hallway light was switched on. Rose squinted in the sudden brightness, holding one hand up to shield her eyes.

She was staring at herself in Gothic clothes, pale foundation and dark lipstick.

Sally broke free and ran up to the other Rose, her tail wagging her whole body as she nuzzled the stranger, sniffing madly. Then she abruptly stopped and looked back at Rose in confusion.

The other Rose held up a finger to her lips, then pointed to the stairs. She turned the hall light off again and Rose followed her in the darkness with Sally sandwiched between them.

As she climbed into the lighted attic, Rose could see her double already sitting on the bed, patting Sally who was still nuzzling her and licking her hands. "Let me have a look at you," she said as Rose approached.

"Please… tell me what's happening here," stammered Rose.

Her 'other self' snorted. "You honestly think I know?" Rose could see that she had a stud in her tongue.

"Well you seem to know a lot more than I do," countered Rose as she took a seat on the other end of the bed.

Her double laughed. "All I did was use the door." She

pointed to the ventilation room. "You just did the same thing. It took you long enough to find it, by the way."

"Who… are you?" stammered Rose.

"I'm you, dummy. You're me. Except I'm three years older – it's 2019 here, in case you were wondering," she replied. "Oh, and our names are different," she added. "I call myself 'Sabina' nowadays."

Rose's middle name was 'Sabina': her parents had given it to her in honour of Nonna – Tony's mother – but Rose had never used it.

"Oh… Okay… Hello Sabina. But I don't understand… How can any of this be possible?"

"Your guess is as good as mine," Sabina replied with a shrug. "Parallel universes or something? I don't know. All I can say is that that, over there -" she pointed to the ventilation room, "is like a doorway that connects our worlds. I only found out a few weeks ago."

"How did you work it out?"

"I'm guessing the same as you: by accident," began Sabina. "I came up to the attic one day to have a look around. Dad always used to be up here and I wanted to figure out why. He's quite secretive, you know? I thought maybe he was doing drugs. Anyway, I didn't find anything, so I went inside the ventilation room. I was poking around in there when the door shut behind me because of the wind. When I opened it, I was suddenly in your house. And it was the middle of the night instead of the middle of the day."

"Hey – that's what just happened to me!" said Rose.

"Yeah well, that's how it always happens. There's like a twelve hour difference – well, three years and twelve hours, in fact. That freaked me out the first time, just like I bet this is freaking you out now. But don't worry: all you need to do is get inside, close the door and open it again – and you'll be back home. It's as simple as that."

"You mean I could go home right now?" asked Rose.

"Mm-hm. It'd only take you a second." Sabina smiled as she patted Sally who was sniffing her dark clothes. "The time difference is handy too – if you're like me and you want to go exploring. I've been going through while you guys have been fast asleep." Rose could smell the cigarette smell from where she was sitting. "Nice dog, by the way."

"Thanks. Her name is Sally," said Rose.

"Sally. I like that. When did you get her?"

"On Saturday. While you were stealing the watch."

"Oh… Hey, I just thought I'd get you something for all the trouble I caused you."

"Yeah well, you got picked up by cameras didn't you? So the cops came around and nearly arrested me."

"Eh? How could they have known it was you?" asked Sabina.

"Because I've been caught before. I'm on their database. The police ran a facial recognition program over the CCTV footage – and 'presto'."

"How could you let yourself get caught? Jeez that's dumb!" Sabina said laughing.

"Yeah well… if you keep stealing, you'll also get caught eventually."

"Nah. I don't do that stuff anymore. I stopped ages ago. I just did it one more time to help you out."

"Yeah well, thanks, but no thanks. I've just been to court. They might put me in jail next time," Rose retorted. "So that's why there isn't going to be a next time."

"Ah… now I understand why you locked the door," mused Sabina.

"Yes – at first I put the wardrobe in front. Then when I told Mum about everything, she put a bolt across the door and locked it properly. She said something was wrong with the place: she didn't know what it was, but she thought it had something to do with Dad going overboard with the gambling. Mum's quite superstitious that way. Say… does your Dad gamble too?"

"He used to. He stopped a few years ago but he was never that badly into it anyway. So tell me: what's the deal with your old man?" asked Sabina.

"Mum kicked him out of the house."

"When was that?"

"Also a few years ago."

"Hm," mused Sabina. "I'm sorry about that. I noticed

all the pictures and stuff were gone from the hallway. That made me sad. And I heard you arguing once with your mum."

"Yeah well. She and I have had our... disagreements."

"I know – I read your novella, don't forget." Sabina reminded Rose. "And I have some idea of how tough it is for you at home. After all, both our mothers drink."

"Yours drinks too?" asked Rose, her eyes going wide.

Sabina nodded. "Sure – what's so surprising about that?"

"Well, for starters, your Dad is still here – and he's not gambling..."

"Well, he's here... in the house. But at the same time he's not – if you know what I mean," Sabina remarked. "He's withdrawn from us completely. He sleeps in the lounge now. And it's not because of Mum's snoring either."

"Yes, I saw. I'm sorry," said Rose.

"Don't be. I've got my own life. I'm studying graphic design at uni. I'm guessing you'll want to do the same. It's heaps of fun. I've got a good circle of friends. I'll be moving out as soon as I can. Dad even bought me a car..."

"Yes, I saw the picture!" Rose exclaimed. "The Hyundai Excel?"

Sabina nodded and laughed. "It's a heap of junk, but

Dad says the engine is good and he's been servicing it in his own fashion – you know how he is! But hey – it gets me around. A lot better than that damn bicycle you're still riding."

"You mean Dad's business is doing well enough for him to buy you a car?"

"Sure – why not? asked Sabina with a frown. "Isn't your Dad still working?"

"I can't say. I haven't seen him in three years. I know his business went belly-up: he lost everything to gambling. Last I heard, Dad was bankrupt and living out of a friend's garage, doing work for cash. He even had to sell his van," said Rose.

"Not his van!"

"Yep," said Rose nodding. "Now Mum's lost her job too – although we think she might get a new one soon."

"Here's hoping. My mother's lost her driving licence again – so she's catching the bus. But she's still working as far as I can tell," Sabina responded.

"Wow… our mums are pretty much the same – but our dads are totally different. How strange is that?" Rose remarked.

"Totally different? I don't know about that," Sabina observed. It seems to me, both our mums drink for a reason – and that reason has a lot to do with our dads."

"Yeah – but my dad has a gambling addiction…" Rose began.

"I really don't think that's why your mother drinks," interrupted Sabina. "Look, I've been watching you guys for a while now. Okay, my father doesn't gamble – at least, not any more – but he has his own obsessions. Now I can't tell you what they are – he's kept them a secret – but it really doesn't matter in the end, does it? Not when he's so... withdrawn. Basically it seems to me that the main reason both our mums drink is that they are unhappy: they're lonely."

"Maybe your father is gambling too but you just don't know it," suggested Rose.

"Nah. His business is doing well. If he were throwing his money away on the horses like your father, we'd know, trust me," replied Sabina.

"So what's his problem then? You must have some idea about his 'secrets'." said Rose. As she said this, she noted, with some relief, that Sally had come back to her and was now curling up at her feet.

Sabina thought about this for a while. "Hm. It's somehow all tied to this room. It's been like some sort of magnet for him for most of the last three years. He's been coming up here all the time – spending hours by himself. He stopped talking to us, doing anything with us as a family. He used to be so romantic too – you know?"

"I think I do. My dad used to be the same," remembered Rose.

"I thought things were starting to get better," said

Sabina. "When late last year, Dad stopped going up to the attic, I thought he and Mum might start to patch things up. But it seems too much water has gone under the bridge. He doesn't need to be in the attic anymore: he's still somewhere else in his mind – even when we're at the dinner table together. Just a couple of weeks ago he moved out of the bedroom and into the lounge. It was then that I realised things weren't ever going to be right. Anyway, one day, when I got home from uni and both my parents were out, I thought I'd come up to the attic and have a good look around: see if he wasn't still sneaking up here. As I said, I thought it might be drugs or something. And that's when I found the door – the one to your world," Sabina said. "At first, I wondered if Dad was using the door – coming to visit you guys. But after reading your journal – going right back to your first entries – I can't see any sign of it."

Rose breathed in deeply and shook her head. "No – if he'd been around, I think we'd have known about it."

"Which is strange, don't you think? If we both found out about the doorway accidentally, then surely my father must have too?" asked Sabina. "Especially since he spent almost three years basically living up here. I mean, all it would have taken is one time – just one time – where he was in the ventilation room checking something and when the door closed behind him."

"Except," interrupted Rose, shaking her head, "that

would never have happened. Not over the last three years anyway."

"Why not?"

"Because three years ago my father decided to seal off the whole wall. He removed the door and put in a panel. We only had a new door fitted at the beginning of the year when the air-conditioner malfunctioned. So you see, the whole time your father was up here doing whatever he was doing, the door between our worlds simply didn't exist."

"And now the door is now finally open again – after all these years," said a deep voice from the staircase.

Both girls turned abruptly to see Tony peering in, his head just above the trapdoor. They froze as he climbed up the remaining steps into the attic. Rose stood up and backed away towards the ventilation room. Sally stood in front of her mistress, ears cocked, the familiar low rumble in her throat. Once he was out, Tony stood near the trapdoor, his tall frame bending under the sloping roof-line, his gaze fixed on Rose. He scanned to Sabina and then back to Rose again. Finally he said, with tears welling in his eyes: "Rose – is that really you sweetheart?"

Collide

The girls looked at each other but Tony's gaze remained fixed on Rose. He stepped forward into the middle of the room which allowed him to straighten up. Rose was surprised to see that he looked almost the same as when she had last seen him three years before: he hadn't seemed to have aged at all.

"It is you. I can hardly believe it…" whispered Tony approaching Rose. Sally stopped her growling and cautiously stepped forward to meet the stranger. He put out the back of his hand for Sally to sniff without taking his eyes off his daughter.

"Um… there are two of us now Dad – and I think you're looking at the wrong one…" said Rose. "Your daughter is over there." She pointed to Sabina. "I've come from another… world – through that door," she said, pointing to the ventilation room.

Tony shook his head slowly, saying: "I came through the door just like you did Rosie. So you see, I'm your real dad. The Tony you've known for the last three years is actually Sabina's father. We swapped places – and then the door stopped working so we couldn't swap back." Rose could see a single tear spill from one of his eyes. He hurriedly wiped it away turning to Sabina to say: "I'm sorry honey but it's true. I've wanted to tell you and your mother from the beginning but I couldn't think of a way of doing it that didn't sound completely mad."

Tony looked back to Rose whose bottom lip was quivering. "I've missed you sweetheart…" he said. When she didn't walk forward, Tony abruptly closed the gap himself, wrapping his arms around her. Initially Rose stood limply, her face hidden against her father's chest. Then she slowly lifted her arms and put them around her father's back, her body racked by silent sobs. They stayed that way for quite some time, both father and daughter clinging to each other in the quiet of the attic, sniffing, while Sally paced around them panting. Sabina watched from the side, wiping the odd mascara-stained tear from her pale cheeks.

Eventually Tony gently released himself from Rose's grasp, kissed her on the forehead and walked over to Sabina, easing himself down on the bed next to her. "Honey, I'm afraid I'm going to have to get straight to the point as we're running out of time." He took one of her hands in his own. "Can you tell me how long the door has been open?"

Sabina sniffed. "I don't know… I've been using it for the last few weeks."

"Have you had any problems getting through?"

"No," answered Sabina. "It seems to work every time."

Tony exhaled and nodded. "That's good. That means there's still a chance."

"For what?" asked Sabina.

"To put things right," he replied.

"Are you leaving us?" Sabina asked.

"I'm afraid so honey. Your father and I weren't meant to swap places. It was after we did that that everything started to go wrong. But now we finally have a chance to put things back to the way they were."

Sabina swallowed. "But... you live here now! Don't you love us?"

"Oh Sabina," said Tony, "of course I love you and your mother! I know I haven't shown you that nearly enough: I'm afraid I've spent three years obsessing about what I'd lost instead of appreciating what I had. That was wrong of me – very wrong. But I can't change what I've done here – just as your father can't change whatever he's done in Rose's world. We both just have to do the best we can from now on."

"Why can't you stay... and do your best here – in this world?"

"My dear Sabina... I wish I had the time to explain. Hopefully it'll all make sense to you soon. For now, please trust me when I say that things can only be fixed –

in this world and in Rose's – if your father and I swap back – as soon as possible."

"What makes you so sure he'll want to?" asked Rose from behind them.

Tony turned around to face her. "I'm not sure Rosie. But I have to do everything in my power to convince him to do it – before it's too late."

"Too late for what?" asked Rose.

"To save him from his gambling addiction."

Rose frowned. "How do you know about that Dad?"

"Let's just say that the way we swapped places tells me a lot about what Sabina's father has been up to in my world. By my calculations, I'd say we have about five days left before he destroys himself completely. Which means that door has re-opened just in the nick of time."

"What if my dad doesn't want to come back?" asked Sabina, a fresh tear appearing on her black-streaked face. "You'll come back then, won't you? I mean, two of you won't want to live in the same world…"

Tony took a deep breath, wiping her cheek with his thumb. "Sabina, I'm promising you now that you'll get your real dad back – one way or another. And when you do, he'll be a better father and husband than I've ever been."

"How can you possibly know that?"

"Because I know that he misses you and your mum – very badly. Don't forget – we're the same person, even if he is three years older. I know exactly how he thinks and feels. And I know that when he sees you, he'll feel exactly what I just felt when I saw Rose," said Tony. "Besides," he said, a smile curling up one corner of his mouth, "I have a plan: one I've spent three years preparing." He pulled her in for a hug. "Trust me," he said quietly, swaying her from side to side as he patted her back. "The father you used to know and love – he'll be back."

"He'd better," said Sabina, her voice wavering. "Or I'll come and get him myself."

Tony abruptly let go, winked at Sabina and headed for the door. "Coming Rosie? Time to go home," he said.

Rose gave Sabina a quick hug and grabbed Sally by the collar. Then together she and her father walked into the ventilation room and closed the door.

They stood for a moment in the darkness. Rose flicked on her torch and shone it up at Tony who shielded his eyes.

"Hey!"

"Sorry Dad." She diverted the beam away from him and shone it around the room: it looked the same as ever. Rose noticed that her father was stooping because of the low rafters – even though he was in the middle of the room where the clearance was at its highest. "What now?" she asked.

"Well… it should work straight away. I usually give it a few minutes just to be sure," Tony replied, "but… this time I think we've waited long enough. Heck – three years is more than long enough. So here it is: the moment of truth. Please try the door love." Rose heard him inhale sharply.

Rose turned around, pulled down on the handle and pushed.

The door didn't budge. She pushed again but it moved a millimetre or so at most.

"Dad – it's stuck. I can't open the door," said Rose, pushing harder. She was about to give up and pull away when Tony rushed forward, grabbing her arm.

"Whatever you do, don't let the handle come back up! Keep pulling it down – and keep pushing!"

"Why? What's happening Dad?"

"The door… it's been locked from the other side."

"So how can we get through?"

"We can't – not unless it's unlocked."

"But we'll be trapped in here!" cried Rose.

"That's one thing you needn't worry about. If you let the handle up and try again, the door will re-open," said Tony.

"Well why don't I just do that?"

"Sweetheart," said Tony with a sigh, "if you do, we'll just end up back with Sabina…"

"Oh…" Rose let that sink in for a moment, her hand

still pulling down on the handle while her shoulder stayed pressed against the door. "Mum must have locked us in!"

"Yes," said Tony. "Now we've got to get her to let us out. Is she still in the attic? Have a listen."

Rose pressed her ear against the door. "I can't hear anything Dad."

"Damn! I had a feeling this wasn't going to be easy. She must be nearby – we need to get her attention. Start shouting. I'll bang. Make sure you keep pressure on both the handle and door at all times – we haven't come this far just to go back to Sabina's world."

"Mum!" screamed Rose through the tiny gap that had opened up. She could see a flash of light. "Mum – it's me! Let me out!"

Tony came up and started banging on the door.

This went on for some time and Rose started to feel her wrist cramping. "Dad – she's not coming. I'm afraid I'll have to let go."

"Don't you dare. Keep shouting." Tony banged even harder.

Eventually they heard a muffled voice. It was Valerie's. "Go away!" she yelled. "Please, just go away – whoever you are! Leave us alone!" Rose heard her mother's voice wavering as it trailed off.

"Mum, it's me – Rose. I'm trapped in here. You have to let me out."

This was followed by silence.

"Mum, can you hear me? I need you to unlock the door. I can't stay in here. Please!"

Still there was no reply.

Suddenly Sally, who had been pacing and panting nervously, started to bark, the sound booming in the tiny room.

"Mum!" shouted Rose, but her voice was drowned out by the barking. "Mum – it's really me. Please... open the door!"

Thankfully Rose could just make out the sound of keys being jingled. Then she heard the padlock click open. After that her mother's muffled voice said: "Sweetie, I know it's you – I can hear Sally – but I can't pull the bolt across. I think you're leaning on the door too hard."

Rose flashed her light up at Tony, blinding him again. "He gestured for her to back off a little bit. Rose did so but kept some pressure on the door for fear of opening the it back to Sabina's world.

Suddenly Sally fell silent. They heard the bolt slide across.

The next thing Rose knew, the door had swung open and she was falling, her hands outstretched as she sprawled onto the crumbling floorboards. She felt a jolt as her chin smacked the ground. She also inhaled a lungful of the musty ancient wood-odour as air was forced into mouth and her nostrils.

"Oh darling – are you okay?" asked Valerie as she kneeled down to help her daughter. "My poor sweetheart… I just saw the door unlocked so I panicked and locked it again. I didn't know it was you. I'm so sorry! Rosie, let me see you. Oh you're bleeding!"

Rose pulled herself up off the ground, feeling the world spin around her. It was daylight again – late afternoon. She could taste iron in her mouth: she'd bitten her lip. She could also feel stinging on her chin. "I'm okay Mum," she said.

Sally came over to investigate, whining softly.

"You've got a big splinter in you," said Valerie. "Hold still and let me pull it out." She reached for her daughter's chin and tugged with the tips of her fingers. Rose felt a something slip out of her skin and Valerie held up a centimetre-long spike of wood. She threw it onto the ground, wiped her hand on her jeans and said: "I'll have to disinfect the wound."

"In a minute Mum – it's not that bad," said Rose.

Valerie sighed and shook her head. "You silly, silly girl!" she scolded. "We locked that room for a reason! What the hell were you doing in there?"

Before Rose could answer, Tony ducked under the door frame and into the attic space. "She was busy finding me," he said.

Valerie stepped back in surprise when she saw him,

her eyes widening.

Tony smiled briefly with one corner of his mouth. "It's good to see you Val. I've missed you. And I want to come home now – if you'll let me."

Re-order

Rose and her father were seated in the kitchen at the breakfast nook, sipping tea. Valerie was doing the same, but leaning on the other side of the kitchen counter. Tony was telling her the whole story, with the occasional interjection by Rose.

"So there I was living in the other world – three years in my future," he continued. "I'd pretty much given up on ever getting home again. The door just wouldn't work: I'd go in, close it and open it up again. But no matter how many times I tried, I couldn't get back here – to my world. In the first few weeks I used to sneak up to the attic two or three times a day to give it a try. After that, I started checking the door a couple of times a week. Then I switched to once or twice a month. Eventually it became every second or third month. Finally, at the start of this year I stopped trying altogether – it seemed pointless."

"That was because the other Tony had sealed the wall," said Valerie, taking a sip of her tea. "There was no door here anymore for you to go through."

"Exactly. I heard Rose telling Sabina about it when I was hiding on the stairs. It confirmed my suspicion that the other Tony had done something deliberately to stop us from swapping back."

"Why would he want to do that?" asked Rose. "Didn't he love his wife and Sabina? They sounded happy enough. Didn't he know he'd miss them?"

"I suppose he thought he was going to be with his family after all – he'd just be going back in time a little. And while they might have been happy enough in the other world, I think the other Tony thought he could make his little family even happier in this one…"

Rose frowned. "Eh? How?"

"Think about it: he would know exactly what was going to happen in the next three years…"

Tony watched as Valerie and Rose exchanged glances.

"Yes: it was all about gambling," he admitted. "And I'm afraid I'm partly to blame for that. You see, I met Sabina's father when I first went through the door. I won't bore you with the story – but we both figured out what was happening pretty quickly, even if we didn't know how it worked. Inevitably we started thinking about how we could use the situation to our advantage. And so we made a plan: we decided that he would dig up all the racing results for the last three years and give them to me. I'd win all the major races and give him half of the money. We'd both be rich."

"But that never happened," mused Valerie.

"No, it didn't."

"Why?" asked Rose.

"Because the other Tony betrayed me. He asked me to meet him in his kitchen one day – when the other Valerie was at work and Sabina was at school. I got up at about 4:30 a.m. and went through the door. It was 4:30 p.m. there. I went down to the kitchen and waited, just as we had arranged. I must have waited a whole hour, but he never showed. When I heard the other Valerie's car pulling into the driveway, I ran up to the attic and tried to go through the door again – but it didn't work anymore. And it hasn't worked since. Until now."

Rose's face lit up as she exclaimed: "That must have been the morning we woke up to find the other Tony working in the attic. I went up and saw that he'd taken off the ventilation room door," she recalled.

"Of course, that would have stopped me straight away. You can't travel through the door if one side is open," explained Tony.

"And after that he sealed the wall permanently," continued Rose. "I remember how he went to Bunnings as soon as it opened and bought a big piece of particle board. He cut it to the right size so as to block the hole made by the door frame. Then he painted the whole thing over with this ghastly peach-coloured paint..." Rose paused for a moment then added: "I don't understand how he could be so greedy… you must hate him for that."

The corner of Tony's mouth curled up in a sad smile. "I've had three long years to think about it Rosie and no, I don't hate him. Because I realise that if our roles had been reversed I'd have done the same thing. We are the same person, after all. You can't go through life hating yourself."

"You mean you would have deserted us if you'd had the chance?" Rose asked.

Tony thought about this as he stroked Sally's ears. Eventually he said: "Gambling addiction… is a kind of illness. I see it now. I have it, Sabina's father has it. However, an illness like that doesn't define who you are. It's what you do about it that counts. Yes, I think that back then – given half a chance – I would have done what Sabina's father ended up doing. I'm not excusing it, but it's more complicated than it looks. The important thing is, I wouldn't do it now. I'm no longer the same person I was. Sabina told you that I don't gamble anymore, didn't she?"

"Yes, she did," said Rose

"It doesn't mean I don't want to gamble. It just means that I choose not to. I don't want my illness to control me – to become me. I want to control it. Life… comes down to choices. Sabina's father made a bad choice – one I'm pretty sure I would have made back then."

There was a period of silence. Eventually Valerie said: "This is an awful lot to take in. If I hadn't seen direct evidence of it – like Rose having a body double and you guys coming out of an empty attic room I'd just locked – I don't think I'd believe a word of it. But now some things are finally starting to make sense."

"Like?" asked Tony.

"Well your story explains how 'you' suddenly aged. On the day 'my husband' was sealing up the attic wall, I thought his hair seemed a bit greyer and thinner and his waistline looked a bit wider. I assumed it was my imagination. In the days and weeks after that, I wondered exactly when my husband had crossed the line from skeptical and cynical to bitter and twisted. I also wondered when he had gone from betting on the odd race to becoming a problem gambler."

"He told us he had a 'cosmic formula' that would help him win big," added Rose.

Tony laughed. "That sounds like something I would have said in other circumstances. Thankfully I got to see what would happen to me if I carried on the way I was going with my gambling. I realised that in three years I would be in his shoes."

"But I thought the other Tony was doing okay when you met him in the 'other world'," remarked Rose.

Tony shook his head. "No, actually. His wife and

daughter didn't know it, but he was already a compulsive gambler. In fact, he was so badly in debt that he was desperate for any solution. Meeting me and discovering the door between our worlds – that must have seemed like a gift from Heaven."

"But he cheated you Dad – and he didn't even need to!"

Tony tilted his head in thought. "Oh, he felt he needed to alright. I didn't know at the time, but winning one or two horse races wasn't going to solve his financial problems. As far as he was concerned, he needed to win big. He certainly couldn't afford to halve his winnings. You see, with his gambler's mindset, he was looking for an instant fix. Swapping places with me was that instant fix."

"It was cruel," observed Rose.

"True. But it was also desperate – the act of someone who is at the third stage of compulsive gambling."

"What are the other stages?" asked Valerie.

"The first is winning. The second stage is, obviously, losing. That's followed by the third stage, desperation, which is where gamblers are willing to lie, cheat, steal – do whatever they can – to get back to the first stage. Then comes the fourth stage, hopelessness – where the gamblers either wind up in jail or commit suicide. The fifth stage – which very few get to – is recovery."

"Hmph," said Valerie. "I don't know where the other

Tony is right now, but I doubt he's at the fifth stage."

"I agree," said Tony. "My guess is that he's probably back at the third stage again – still clutching his last few race results, hoping they'll save him. Ironically, he's just gone full circle – repeating the first three stages all over again in the last three years. The race results helped him do that. He's just spent three years re-creating the mess he left behind in his own world."

"How do you know he has any race results left at all?" wondered Valerie.

"Well, we swapped places in the early hours of Monday the fourth of November in this world – the day before the Melbourne Cup. In the other world it was the evening of the twelfth of November 2016."

"Hold on – Sabina told me the time difference between the worlds was three years and twelve hours," said Rose.

"Not quite. It's exactly three years, eight days and twelve hours – give or take a minute," replied Tony. "It's because of those extra days that the other Tony knew the results from this Melbourne Cup racing season. But those extra days are running out. Today is the seventh of November – so he has, at most, five more days of race results to try. He'll have them written down in a book he keeps in his back pocket…"

"I know the one!" exclaimed Rose. "I remember how he used to keep checking the online results against it!"

Tony nodded. "Exactly Rosie. So he's still got some hope of winning big. And that's what's going to keep him at stage three for at least a few days more. After that… who knows?"

"And what stage are you at?" asked Valerie.

Tony smiled with one corner of his mouth. "I was at stage two when I was still here: I was losing all the time, but pretending it was fine – just a hobby – when inside I was starting to become obsessed about winning. Thanks to the other Tony, I saw how my future was going to pan out. I knew I had to do everything in my power to avoid that happening. So I skipped the other stages and went straight to number five."

Valerie frowned. "How?"

"By joining Gamblers' Anonymous. They really helped me. It was a slow road. Actually it *is* a slow road – I'll probably be on it for the rest of my life. But I'm okay with that."

Valerie nodded. "And what about the other Tony's debts? In this world, I had to do some pretty hard work to insulate Rose and me from his gambling. Lucky I'm a family law specialist and we split before things got really bad. I don't know how you managed to keep his business afloat in the other world."

"Oh boy – his business…" Tony combed his hair back. Rose noticed it was thinning and grey – but no more so than when she had last seen him three years previously. "That was hard work," continued her father. "I saw a good financial planner and got a low interest loan to consolidated and refinance all the debts. Then I worked double shifts, scrimped and saved – basically I did whatever I had to. Because of that, I paid off the last of the other Tony's debts a few weeks ago. But the stress nearly killed me. I decided to keep everything a secret from the other Valerie and Sabina. That, along with the fact that I spent nearly all my 'spare' time thinking about you guys and trying to get back to you through the ventilation room door... Well, let's just say that while I saved other Tony's business, I didn't save his marriage. In fact, I let it fall apart. I didn't see the warning signs of the other Valerie's increased drinking. I could have helped her – and I should have helped her – but I didn't." He drained his cup of tea and put it down.

"I'm going to go out on a limb and say that you're being too hard on yourself," said Valerie. "You're a good man Tony. At the same time, I hope you realise that you can't just walk back into our lives and pick things up from where they left off. Too much has happened."

"I know that. But I'm here. And I'm willing to give it a try. That's as much as I can do."

Valerie sighed. "Well right now we have a more immediate problem as far as I can see. What are we going to do about the fact that there are two of you here now? That's not really workable in the long-term is it? I hate to get all 'legal' on you, but you can't share Medicare cards, tax file numbers…"

"As I told Sabina, I have a plan."

"You and your plans!" scoffed Valerie.

"Seriously – I might not know about a lot of stuff, but I'm a bona fide expert on Tony Azzopardi. I'm sure even you'd agree with that." He winked.

Valerie laughed. "Okay, so where do we start?"

"It has to do with the bets he's going to place in the next five days," replied Tony. "And I'm going to need your help Rosie."

"I'm so glad we're doing this," said the other Tony to Rose.

They were seated at a table at Valentino's and he was holding her hand over the table. It was the day after she had brought her real father back into her world. Rose had called the other Tony's mobile number for the first time in three years and arranged to have coffee after school.

"I'm glad too Dad."

"It's been way too long – eh? And look at you – all grown up," he said. Rose noticed that he was visibly older: new lines scored his face and those that she already knew were deeper – in particular the two lines between his eyebrows. He'd also gained weight. Apart from anything else, he looked tired: bone-tired – as if he'd just finished a long shift at Valentino's.

"Have you been working?" she asked.

"Yeah, you know: cash-only. But my bankruptcy ends in about a month so I'll be able to start up properly again then. It'll be good. Say, how's your mother?"

"She's okay. Moving to a new job soon."

"Oh?" he raised an eyebrow.

"What?"

"Nothing," said the other Tony, shaking his head and taking a sip of his coffee. "Tell your mum I miss her, okay?"

"Well she misses you."

"Oh I bet," he said, a smirk at one corner of his mouth.

"No, she really does."

He snorted. "Tell me: is she drinking? I bet that's why she's looking for a new job."

"Dad!" exclaimed Rose, pulling away.

He held his hands up. "My bad – I shouldn't have mentioned it. I came here to have a quiet cup of coffee and reconnect with my daughter – not talk about Val's problems." Rose looked away and the other Tony sat in silence for a while. "So this is where you work?" he asked eventually.

"Uh-huh."

"Do they treat you well?"

"Yeah – not too bad."

"And school?"

"I've had two exams already. I have two more on Thursday and one next week."

"How do you feel about them?"

"Yeah – I should be fine."

"That's my girl," he said with a chuckle. "You were always a smart cookie. Hard-working too."

Rose smiled weakly. "Dad, I'm just going to go to the loo."

"Of course. Catch you in a minute eh?" He grinned as he watched his daughter get up and walk to the corridor. A minute passed as he sipped his coffee, surveying the afternoon crowd.

Then suddenly he saw a younger version of himself walking purposefully towards his table.

Rose saw it all playing out from the corridor: her father approaching the other Tony and pulling up a chair, Tony's smile and the shocked look on the older man's face. At that moment Evan came up from behind Rose and surprised her.

"I didn't know your dad had a twin!" he exclaimed.

"Um – yeah. He does," she replied absently, still looking at the pair, trying to read their lips but failing – they were simply too far away.

"I'm sorry to say that your dad doesn't look too happy to see his brother," Evan pointed out. He was noticing that the other Tony was leaning back with his arms crossed, ignoring his 'brother's' extended a hand.

"They haven't spoken in years," murmured Rose.

"Oh wow... Say – did you set this up?"

"Let's just say that I played my part," Rose said, still studying the pair intently.

"That's pretty special. Do you mind me asking what went wrong between them? You can tell me to buzz off if it's too personal."

"Nah – it's just the usual, you know: money."

"That's sad," said Evan. When he fell silent, Rose turned around and noticed Evan was looking at her curiously.

"What?" she asked.

"You once told me that your relationship with your father was 'broken forever'. So when I heard you were having coffee with your dad, I assumed it was about you guys reconnecting, not..."

"Oh," Rose waved her hand, "I didn't tell you, but Dad and I patched things up over the last couple of days. He even saw mum yesterday. We're all good. Now it's time to fix another relationship: one that's been broken way too long." She turned back to watch her father and his older counterpart.

"I've got to hand it you Rosie," said Evan as he walked away. "You never cease to surprise me." Rose noticed he was using her nickname. She looked up in time to see him wink.

"What the hell are you doing here?" said the older man through gritted teeth.

The hand that was extended towards him wavered and was eventually withdrawn. Tony leaned back in his chair and replied: "The door – it's open again."

"How? Never mind – we swapped years ago. This is my world now – and you don't belong in it." The older man glanced around the room. "What will people think when they see two of us?"

"That we're twins," answered Tony, shrugging. "I mean we are clearly identical – it's just that you're obviously looking worse for wear."

"Shut the hell up. I'm here to reconnect with Rose. She finally called me after three long years and now you've come to wreck everything. You'd better get lost before she comes back from the toilets."

"Why?" asked Tony.

The older man sighed. "For obvious reasons, you bastard. She'll see that there are two of us. She knows I don't have a twin."

"Yeah well, I wouldn't worry about Rose. She knows."

"She what?" The other Tony leaned forward, his eyes widening.

"Like I told you," Tony said calmly. "She knows. All

of it."

"How?"

Tony also leaned over the table and said quietly: "Our daughters discovered the door together."

"Well if you want us to swap back, you can forget it," hissed his double.

"Is that because you left me up shit creek without a paddle?"

"You're damn right," spat back the older man.

"From what I hear, you've stuffed things up on this side as well."

"Not for long. My big payday is coming up soon. And sorry, I'm not sharing it with you. That's just the way the cookie crumbles," said the other Tony.

The younger man sighed and shook his head. "Okay… What if I had something to offer you in return?"

His double scoffed. Then abruptly his eyes narrowed and he leaned in too. "What are we talking about here — more race results?" Beads of sweat were forming on his brow and he dabbed at them with his napkin, then combed his hair back with his hand.

Tony nodded. "Fresh ones. You'll have noticed that the older ones you have are getting more and more unreliable. You wouldn't be bankrupt if they weren't."

There was a moment of silence as the older man thought this through. Eventually he said: "Yeah, well —

some of the results haven't worked out. So what? Our worlds aren't identical. But there's a race this weekend that was big for me last year and the year before – I just didn't have enough capital. This time, I do."

Tony sighed. "As you wish. In that case, I'll just play with my fresh race results. We both know the first results are the most accurate. Remember Melbourne Cup 2013? Fiorente, Red Cadeaux, Mount Athos and Simeon? You never quite matched that win did you? I mean, how did this year's Melbourne Cup go for you?"

The other Tony's mouth opened but he didn't reply.

"Just as I figured. You lost. Now if only you'd bet the house, the car – everything – on that one first race… Instead you only put down a couple of hundred. Tsk, tsk. What a waste, eh? Oh well. Have a nice life…" Tony started to get up but his double grabbed him.

"Okay. What are you suggesting?" hissed the older man.

"Same deal we made originally: we split the money evenly, except this time, you keep your word – and we swap back," Tony answered, looking down at the white knuckles digging into his forearm.

"Why would you want to do that? I mean, if you have the numbers, why not play them by yourself and use the money in the other world?"

"Because," said Tony, "I want to come home. Those are my terms. Take them or leave them."

"This is some sort of trick isn't it? You want to lure me into the ventilation room and close the door," the older man said, clinging to Tony's arm.

"You're afraid I'm going to betray you the way you betrayed me eh? Well you're wrong," said Tony.

"So I'm just supposed to trust you? As if! I wonder why you're so desperate to swap back... How bad must things be over there?"

Tony laughed. "I can tell you now, they're a hell of a lot better than they are here. For starters, Val and I are living under the same roof – in different rooms, but still. And the business is also running – no thanks to you."

"It can't be... You're up to something," the other Tony said.

Tony sighed again. "Listen – all I want is to go home. I bet you do too. Because whichever way you look at it, the Valerie you know here isn't your wife. And that girl," he said pointing to the corridor, "isn't your child. As you said, our worlds aren't identical. We've both been in the wrong place for three years. It's time to put things right. The ball's in your court." As he finished saying this, Tony placed his hand over his older counterpart's which was still clutching his forearm.

"Okay... what do you want me to do?"

"Go home. Eat something. Take a shower. Come to Val's after dinner. Say 8:30 p.m. We'll chat then," answered Tony.

"Val knows?" the older man asked, his eyes widening. "She knows."

Rose was watching as these events played out. Evan, who was passing by carrying empty plates, said: "Well it seems you've fixed another broken relationship – look." He gestured at the two men holding each other's arms across the table.

"Not quite yet. But I think we're making progress," she replied. At that moment Rose looked down at her hands. She realised she hadn't washed them at all that day. And it didn't bother her one bit.

Rose was looking through the lounge window when she saw the car pulling in: an old battered van with a hand-painted sign that said 'AirCon4U – Cheap' and a mobile number below that. She watched the other Tony get out, slam the door and walk up the gravel path onto the porch. Sally barked.

"He's here," she said to Valerie and Tony. There was a knock on the door.

"Bring him to the dining room Rosie," said Valerie.

A moment later they were all seated around the table. Rose had made a pot of tea and everyone was sipping from cups – except the visitor who sat stony-faced and arms crossed, slouching in his chair. He even ignored

Sally who was trying to get his attention, sniffing and trying to lick his hands. "Okay, enough with the pleasantries," he said. "What have you got for me?"

"A chance to start a new life – for both of us," answered Tony.

"What are we talking – the results for the Boxing Day races at Caulfield?"

"No, not that," said Tony.

"You're kidding me? Tell me you picked another big race day!"

"I didn't pick any race day."

The other Tony laughed – a humourless laugh – then shook his head. "You're trying to trick me after all."

"I'm not."

"What do you take me for?"

"A gambler," answered Tony.

The older man scoffed. "You and me both."

"That's true. We'll be gamblers for the rest of our lives. Just as Val here is always going to be an alcoholic.

"Hey!" exclaimed Valerie.

"Sorry honey, but it's true. We are who we are. But that's not what's important – it's what we do about it that counts."

"Oh spare me!" exclaimed the other Tony. "Where did you get this shit? Dr. Phil?"

"No – I've been going to Gamblers Anonymous for three years now," answered the younger man.

"Well good for you!"

"Actually it's good for both of us. Because I stopped gambling, I was able to save your air-conditioning business – the one you ran into the ground back in the other world," said Tony. "And I'm happy to give it to you. In return I just want my own world back – in whatever state you've left it."

"What a moron you are! You said it yourself: all you needed were fresh race results. You could have brought them with you. Instead you bring me psychobabble and a pathetic business that's probably sinking – if it's even still afloat. I have had enough of this," said the other Tony getting up.

"Where are you going?" asked Valerie.

"Back to the garage where I'm currently living. But guess what? I'll only be there for the rest of the week. Come Saturday, I'm going to rake in the biggest payday ever. And after that, I'll be living in a mansion. When that happens, you," he said pointing at Valerie, "are going to be very sorry you ever doubted me!"

"Do you really believe that – or do you just want to believe that? Because there's a difference," said Tony.

"Shut up," said the older man. "A few race results – that's all you needed to bring with you. You couldn't even do that."

"What good would they have done?" asked Tony.

"You said yourself – they would have been fresh!

Fresh results work best!"

Tony shook his head sadly. "You just don't get it do you? The only 'fresh' results we were ever going to have were the very first ones you tried. Any results after that were bound to become less and less accurate. The results in your back pocket are already three years old! They aren't reliable any more. Any new ones I might have brought over would have been even less reliable!"

The other Tony grimaced and said: "What the hell are you talking about?"

"Exactly what we talked about three years ago when we made our first deal: Chaos Theory. Our two worlds used to be identical, running side by side, like parallel lines. But from the moment we found the door between our worlds, those lines started to drift apart. We introduced a small angle. At the beginning, the lines would have still been pretty close to each other. But the more time has passed, the further they have moved away from each other."

"Pah!" the older man spat out. "You and your damn Chaos Theory."

"It's not my theory," snapped Tony. "You know as much about it as I do. The gambler in you just wants to ignore that."

"I don't have time for theories. I'm a practical man."

"Listen to me!" shouted Tony. "We changed history in both worlds. Why would you expect the race results from one to work in the other?"

"Give me a break," said the older man. "How could some trivial changes to one small family household possibly affect horse racing results on the other side of the country?"

"You know the 'Butterfly Effect' as well as I do," Tony replied.

"What is that?" asked Valerie.

"Basically it goes something like this: even a butterfly flapping its wings in China can cause a series of changes that eventually result in a tornado tearing its way through the American Midwest." Tony turned to his older double, adding: "And we know it works because you should be a billionaire. Yet you aren't."

The other Tony thought about this for a while, sitting in the silence of the dining room. Rose could hear the buzzing of the fridge and the clicking of the 1970s clock in the hall. Eventually their guest sighed and said: "All I know is, I've got a set of results in my pocket for a race that's always been good to me. I'm not going to blow my last chance on some 'theory'." He got up, saying: "I should have known you were trying to trick me." Then he began walking to the front door.

Valerie looked at Tony in desperation and said: "So this was your great plan eh?"

"I thought I could reason with the bastard!" exclaimed Tony. "We're the same person after all! I even saved his damn business!"

"You told me yourself: he's a stage three compulsive gambler – reason was never going to work," said Valerie shaking her head.

As they heard the front door handle being pulled, Tony abruptly jumped up and ran into the lounge calling: "Hey! Wait up!"

"I really don't want to hear any more BS from you," said the other Tony. "Go back to the other world. There's only room for one of us here."

"Before I do, just tell me this: the race you're banking on," said Tony, "I'm guessing it's the Ladbroke Sandown Cup – over 3,200 metres." Rose and Valerie had appeared behind him as he said this.

His older double paused at the open door. "Yeah – so?"

"Is Vautour in the field?"

With a sigh, the other Tony reached into his back pocket and pulled out his notebook. "I think so – let me see." He flicked through the pages, licking his thumb as he searched until he eventually found the correct place. "Yes – he is." He sneered as he put the book into his back pocket. "So what?"

"So you obviously missed the news," replied Tony.

"What news?"

"Vautour just broke his foreleg on Sunday. It was a freak accident at Mullins' yard. They had to put the horse down."

"You're lying!" the older man exclaimed.

"I saw it on TV this morning. Take a look at the racing news on your phone – you'll see I'm telling the truth."

Even from the lounge, Rose could see beads of sweat forming on the other Tony's forehead as he pulled out his phone and began tapping. His breathing became heavy and he shook his head. "You bastard," he said quietly, "you're right…"

"See – your results aren't reliable anymore."

The older man combed the wet strands of hair backwards with a shaky hand. "I've borrowed money… The race might pan out differently…"

"That's what I've been trying to tell you," implored Tony.

The four of them stood in silence for a few moments, with the other Tony staring blankly at the floor until he suddenly took a deep breath and said: "Well… I didn't have Vautour in the top four, so it won't matter. Anyway, I can't trust you – you're probably lying about my business. I'll just have to take my chances with the results I have." He pushed on the screen door and stepped outside.

"Wait Dad!" called a voice from the staircase. Sally barked again and began to rush forward, but Valerie grabbed the dog's collar. She, Tony and Rose looked at each other in confusion. The pressure on Sally's throat made her cough as she strained forward.

The screen door reopened and the other Tony walked back into the foyer, frowning in puzzlement as he peered up towards the attic. "Who said that? Rose? Is that… *my* Rosie? Can it really be you…?" Tears began to well in his eyes.

The others heard the heavy sound of Doc Martens boots on the stairs and eventually Sabina stepped into view. "Yeah Dad – it's me," she said. "I heard what you said before. Please – don't risk everything on that race. Take a chance on us instead," she said. "We miss you. It's time you came home."

Live

"Well, that's certainly an amazing story you have there – and the drawings are stunning. Thanks for sharing this with me," said Patricia, handing the journal back to Rose. It was the twenty-second of December – her last appointment with the psychiatrist.

"I'm glad you liked it," Rose replied.

"You know, I'm very proud of you. Somehow you've turned a major life crisis into an engaging work of art. And you've been so inventive too – adding all those sci-fi elements... That was incredible. It's a very positive way of dealing with your issues – and a very brave way too."

"Thanks," said Rose, stuffing her journal back into her backpack.

"I particularly liked how you created this fantastical, parallel way in which your parents got back together. It's magical. Have they seen your journal?"

"Yeah – I showed them a while back."

"What did they think?"

"Mum cried. Dad says he's proud of me."

"So… how is their relationship going?" asked Patricia.

"Baby steps, you know."

"Do you mind me asking if they are sharing a bedroom again?"

Rose laughed. "Yes – finally. Dad moved back in with Mum after she saw a sleep specialist at the QEII Medical Centre. They discovered she had quite bad sleep apnoea. She had to have surgery to remove her adenoids and tonsils. That was about a week ago. It's heaps better now. And Dad can finally get some sleep."

"Wonderful! What about your mother's drinking?"

"Dad's taking Mum to her AA meetings. Mum's going with Dad to his Gamblers Anonymous meetings… They both seem to be doing okay."

"I'm happy to hear it. Now what about your father's work?"

"Well, his bankruptcy period ended on Monday, so I've spent the week helping him respray his van. Dad's also got a new business name and I designed a logo which we're putting on his vehicle as well as on his business cards and letterheads. Lately, we've been working on his website. There's a lot to do. It's a good thing I've got school holidays. Basically, we get started as soon as Dad drops Mum off at her new job. But most nights we try to stop an hour before Mum gets back so he and I can cook together. It feels like the old days."

"That's lovely Rose! And you? I see your own

compulsions have faded."

"How can you tell?" asked Rose.

"Your fingers – the skin isn't split any more from over-washing your hands."

"Oh. Yeah – I stopped that a while back. As well as the counting and everything else."

"How did you manage it?"

"I've worked out that life is all about choices. It's like I said in my story: I didn't want my compulsions to own me – to become me. So I chose to control them," said Rose

"You make it sound easy," said Patricia.

Rose smiled with one corner of her mouth – just like her father. "It definitely wasn't easy. But that's life, you know? There isn't an easy road – they're all hard. You just have to pick one and work at it."

"Well, I hope you and your dad will at least take some time off now that Christmas is coming. Do you have anything planned for the holidays?" asked Patricia.

"We have a family dinner on Christmas eve – the first one in three years."

"You, your mum and dad, I suppose." The psychiatrist smiled. "And, of course, Sally."

Rose blushed. "Well… Evan's coming over too."

"My, my! How does he get along with your father?"

"Too well!" said Rose, laughing. "They spent an entire Saturday pulling out the old dead jarrah tree from the front yard. They've replaced it with a sapling – a Norfolk Island pine."

"And let me guess – your dad's going to put Christmas lights on it?"

Rose laughed again. "Yep – he's doing it as we speak. I think Evan's there now, helping him. Actually, he and Dad are planning to decorate the whole outside of the house. It's going to be the most amazing light show in the street – even fancier than the Chiongs'. Dad can get quite competitive."

"Speaking of the Chiongs, did you ever make up with Jen and Jon?"

"Um… no."

"Does that bother you?"

"Yes and no."

"Care to elaborate?"

Rose thought about it for a while before she answered: "I wanted to be friends with them – I really did. They seem like nice people. But in the end, you can't make everyone like you. Some things are beyond your control. This is one of them."

Outside Patricia's office Rose faced the fresh sea breeze, combing strands out of her hair as she put on her helmet. She was thinking about how she would soon be riding into her driveway where three cars would be parked. Music might be wafting from the lounge –

Leonard Cohen most probably – along with the sounds of conversation and laughter and the smell of her mum's chicken tikka masala. The Christmas lights might even be up. Sally would prance around her as if she'd been away for months.

Or... maybe her father would still be balancing on a ladder, shouting instructions to Evan, trying to work out why the lights weren't working yet while mosquitoes buzzed in their ears. Her tired and cranky mum might have burned the chicken tikka masala so they'd end up having to order pizza. Sally would, of course, be prancing regardless.

Either situation would be fine. Because in life you don't always get what you want. You just have to make the best of what you have.

With that thought, she smiled and set off into the late afternoon sunshine.

Notes

I was sitting at my dining room table opposite my daughter Maya (aged ten) one Sunday morning in late October this year. We were eating breakfast. As I recall, I was reading the news on my phone.

Maya said: "Dad, you know how you write a lot of books…"

"Uh-huh," I mumbled, not really listening as I was reading about the up-coming US election.

"How come you never write anything we can read?" By 'we' Maya was referring to herself and her older sister Lara (aged fourteen).

I put the phone down. I didn't really know how to reply. It was a good question – especially since I'd always maintained that my main ambition in life was to write books for young adults. Yet all the books I'd written up to that point had been so very… 'older adult'.

In that very instant, I decided I had to stop making excuses. Yes, it was getting close to the end of the year and yes, I was busy at work finishing things up – blah, blah, blah… but none of that mattered. I wasn't going to delay it a moment longer: I was going to start writing a book that my daughters could read and enjoy. It had to be something they could relate to – something I would have wanted to read at their age (and would still want to read today).

So I said "Okay Maya – what kind of story would you like?"

"It has to be a mystery," she replied.

"A mystery eh?"

"Do you know anything about mysteries?" she asked.

"Mm – a little."

"Because it has to be done right," Maya told me. "Like, it should be set in a dark, spooky place… maybe an attic."

I immediately searched my phone for images of dark spooky attics. One of the pictures that came up caught my eye. It was a photograph by Karl-Heinz Spremberg. That photograph – which is now on the cover – was my sole inspiration (I bought the rights to use it, in case you were wondering).

'Girl in the Attic' was then written in nightly instalments, each published in a blog over the following six weeks (see http://girlintheatticnovel.blogspot.com).

I had quite a ride. I hope you enjoyed it too.

Dan Djurdjevic
22 December 2016

Thanks

Thank you to my wife Maureen, my daughters Maya and Lara, and my good friends Dave, Daphne, Ian, Alison and Shelly B.